THE **LAKE** OF THE **BEGINNING**

THE **LAKE** OF THE **BEGINNING**

ED GRAY

WILLOW CREEK PRESS
Minocqua, Wisconsin

Published by Willow Creek Press

P.O. Box 147

Minocqua, Wisconsin 54548

Designed by Heather M. McElwain

For information on other Willow Creek titles, call 1-800-850-9453

Library of Congress Cataloging-in-Publication Data
Gray, Ed.
    The lake of the beginning / Ed Gray.
      p.   cm.
    ISBN 1-57223-085-1
    I. Title.
PS3557.R2923L35   1998   98-30023
813'.54--dc21   CIP

Printed in Canada

To Caroline, Douglas, Hope, Sam and Will.

ACKNOWLEDGMENTS

First and foremost this text is entirely a work of fiction. None of the characters in this tale can be found in any written history, and there are no native people, past or present, called Qualik. The creation myth to be found here is to be found here only, for the first time I heard it, as the old people would say, was when I told it to myself. But no story springs fully formed from any-thing like a void, and this is true especially of this narrative. I am deeply indebted to all the nameless storytellers in the North Coast Inuit and all the other Native American traditions, and very specifically to Peter John of Minto, Alaska and Gilbert Sewell of Pabineau Falls, New Brunswick, Athabascan and Micmac respectively, each of whom taught me in his own way the value of a question when pressed for an answer. My gratitude extends as fully to Professor Stephen Hawking for permission to use so critical a kernel from his elegant A Brief History of Time *and to Roger Caras whose lovely* Sockeye: The Life of a Pacific Salmon *planted the seed of this story twenty years before it ripened.*

— Ed Gray, May 1998

"As he moved through the water he created his own complex pattern of eddies. Upstream falls and rapids were no more dynamic than these, and no more complicated. The fact that they were in miniature simply suited the scale of the animal itself. As he grew, the currents and eddies he would create with each move would increase and blend in with the billions of others created by all the other creatures in the lake or the sea. No one has ever reckoned the role of these in the movements of the Cosmos, how such energy blends with all others so released and how they play upon each other. This much is certain though: with his exquisite sensory equipment Nerka could read those currents created by the creatures around him and judge their worth, judge their peril. Even as he created currents and sent water particles swirling against each other and in concert against other forms of life, he interpreted second by second those that returned to him from other sources. As he moved with other fish, they communicated by the gentle pressures that the movement of each exerted on all others. When we think of the fish, we must think of this, the degree to which it is locked in step with the Cosmos as well as with smaller wonders. It is all one, and Nerka a part of it."

—Roger Caras,
in *Sockeye: The Life of a Pacific Salmon*

"*Everything an Indian does is in a circle, and that is because the power of the world always works in circles, and everything tries to be round.*"

—Black Elk (Hehaka Sapa),
in *Black Elk Speaks, Being the Life Story of A Holy Man of the Oglala Sioux*

"Even if there is only one possible unified theory, it is just a set of rules and equations. What is it that breathes fire into the equations and makes a universe for them to describe? The usual approach of science of constructing a mathematical model cannot answer the questions of why there should be a universe for them to describe. Why does the universe go to all the bother of existing?"

—Stephen Hawking, in *A Brief History of Time*

S he was beauty itself and against the cold flow she came, urgent as life, relentless as death. She swam with ghosts and she had no name.

She swam, ceaselessly. Endless strength and the grace of pure motion were all that she knew and they propelled her without thought through a turbulent, chaotic realm of underwater noises and overlapping, distant vibrations. Constant hunger and sudden evasion were the only sensations she had ever felt. She had never been asleep.

In the liquid darkness that surrounded her were sleek, undulating shapes and forms almost identical to her, mirrors in space and time that moved with her, and she with them. Waves of energy pulsing from all the nearby propulsion swept across and through her with a gathering harmony that soothed and excited her in ways she had never sensed and over which she had no control. Galvanized and accelerating, lifted from the unlit depths of the ocean in a rising tide of shimmering silver, she swam toward daylight.

Riding an updraft of warming air on wide black wings, a lone raven flew above the cold northern ocean. The raven looked down at the saltwater below and saw a swimming pod of sockeye salmon. Perfectly reflected in the bird's ancient, glittering eye, the fish weren't silver at all, but were instead dark, shaded and packed together so tightly that even to the keen gaze of the raven the pod seemed more like a single giant sea creature just under the surface, inexorable and directed, steadily progressing to the east.

With a loud *cr-r-uck* that carried away and disappeared into the endless sky, the raven flew on, pushing with its wings to hold altitude and flying in silence until the sound of its own voice came back to the bird, hollow and distant, echoing from somewhere far away. Somewhere to the east.

The raven banked and turned that way. Passing once again over the dark pod of salmon, now going in the same direction, the raven flew on.

Soon the raven came upon a rocky, desolate shoreline and an estuary where a small, wild river flowed into the ocean. Crossing over the shore, the raven flew inland, upstream against the river into an expanding landscape of dense forest, hardened mountaintops and sparkling waters, a wild country that seemed to go on forever, that seemed to grow from a limitless horizon, endlessly unfolding ahead of the flying raven, inventing itself from an unseeable beginning and an unknowable place.

The land grew. Great tracts of evergreen trees — spruces and hemlocks, western red cedar and yellow cypress — spilled down from the jagged mountains, giving way along the streams and bogs to cottonwoods and willows, shrubby alders and an occasional stunted growth of silver firs. Cranberries, huckleberries, salmonberries, strawberries and raspberries tangled sunlit openings and boggy edges. Meadows and stream banks blossomed with violets, daisies, lace flower, wintergreen, lilies and sweet gale. Tundra slopes spilled over with yellow heather, alpine azaleas, bellflowers, fernleaf goldthread and bluebells.

The raven looked down and saw shapes moving on the land: mountain goats and black-tailed deer, porcupines and weasels, river otters and squirrels, beavers, minks, muskrats, rabbits, foxes and wolves, black bears and brown bears.

Above the animals, small birds flitted, dipped and cruised. Hummingbirds, swallows, magpies, jays, chickadees, warblers, sparrows and wrens moved through the trees. Loons, herons, snipe, kingfishers, ducks and plovers fed in the shallow ponds. Ptarmigan and grouse walked on the ground. And far behind the raven, rising into the growing sky, soared hawks, falcons and eagles.

The day grew long and the raven flew on, following the valley up into higher land against the river's downhill flow as it tumbled through narrow gorges, sliced through gentle meadows of sedge grass and purled over gravelled shallows. The raven looked up from the river.

Ahead in the distance, glinting in the late afternoon sun like an emerald dropped in a midsummer pasture, lay a quiet lake with green water, surrounded by deep forest. It was the beginning of the river, and the raven flew directly toward it.

On the shore of the green lake the raven's gaze came upon an indistinct human figure — an old man hunkered down next to a tiny fire. Flying toward the solitary human, the raven selected a tall spruce tree nearby and soundlessly landed on its topmost branch, all the while keeping its gleaming eye fixed on the silent, motionless old man. The old man never moved, not even once to look at the raven perched above him, watching carefully.

A long time passed. Night did not come. Smoke from the small fire drifted quietly upward into an odd, unchanging twilight that seemed as if it would last forever. Neither the raven nor the old man shifted position. The small fire glowed, barely burning. Nothing else changed, nothing else moved, except for the quiet drift of wood smoke toward the half-lit sky above. Time seemed neither to go forward nor back.

Finally, the old man moved. Bending just slightly down, he pursed his lips and blew gently on the fire he had made. The small embers glowed, then danced into flames that crackled and sparked, reflecting in the old man's very dark eyes as the fire grew. His eyes glinting and alert, sharp and carefully focused, the old man lifted his head and looked directly at the raven. The raven's eyes were almost identical to the old man's as the bird looked back at him. Their eyes were fixed as they gazed at each other.

A distant sound, droning and faint, slowly spread itself across the waters of the lake. Neither the raven nor the old man looked away from the other.

The sound grew as its source approached. Still the man and the bird did not move. The droning sound now filled the valley, insistent and demanding, coming closer and closer. With his eyes still on the raven, the old man whispered something, one word only that was too faint to be heard above the droning. The raven opened its wings, lifted off from its high perch, and flew away. The old man watched the bird until it was gone and he turned his head toward the oncoming sound.

At the other end of the small lake, coming up the valley and just now appearing over the shoreline spruce trees against a backdrop of steeply rising tundra hills that formed the valley, an airplane appeared. It was a small plane, a four-seat float plane with pontoons, and now it slowed and began to settle toward the lake, coming in for a landing on the water.

The airplane landed in the middle of the lake, gliding smoothly to a stop and rocking gently on the waves it had made on the water's surface. The plane turned away from the shore where the old man's campfire quietly burned — now without any sign of the old man himself — and taxied toward the beach on the opposite side of the lake.

Eons of cracking ice and beating rain had fractured the ancient boulders that had made up this short stretch of lake shore, grinding and smoothing them into a uniform layer of smaller, rounded and flattened stones that the float plane's pontoons now came to rest against with an aluminum scrape on shifting wet gravel. The engine stopped and the droning sound that had come with it fled toward the tops of the surrounding tundra hills, disappearing over them and leaving behind the kind of silence that could almost be felt, a quiet so deep that it seemed to carry a constant echo even though there was no sound to create one. The reverberant silence of wilderness and vast spaces once again settled over the green lake.

The airplane's passenger door opened and out came a woman in her late thirties. Two thousand miles lay between her home in the city and this green lake, but she was no stranger to wild places. Her camping clothes were well-worn and she handled herself deftly as she stepped onto the still-rocking pontoon of the airplane and then ashore without getting her feet wet. In her hands she carried a small package. She moved a few steps away from the airplane before she stopped and slowly scanned the surrounding hills, the uninhabited shoreline and the quiet lake itself. Around her neck and under her shirt, hung on a fine leather thong as soft and supple as worn suede, a very old beartooth amulet lay quietly against her skin, its finely carved edges worn smooth long before the woman had even been born. Almost imperceptibly she nodded, touched the amulet through the cloth of her shirt and took a long, slow breath as she reverently cradled the package.

"Well," she whispered. "You did say it would be beautiful, didn't you?"

Peering out the door behind her were a young boy and girl, her children; the boy was 10 years old and his sister 12. The woman looked back at the airplane.

"Come on out," she said to the children. "This is the place."

The boy came first, elbowing past his sister and squirming through the door as she moved out of his way.

"Hey!" she said in annoyance at him. "Who said you got to be first?"

"Nobody said I couldn't," he answered as he clambered off the pontoon and splashed through the ankle-deep water onto the beach. His sister shook her head at him and shrugged, then climbed carefully down onto the pontoon and stepped forward along it until she could reach the shore without getting her feet wet, just as she had watched her mother do. Together they stood and looked at the placid, immense wilderness that surrounded them.

"Wow," said the girl in a hushed voice. "I didn't know it would be like this."

"I did," said her brother. "It's just like the books Mom showed us. Didn't you even look at them?" He picked up a flat stone and threw it sidearm out into the water. It sank without skipping and he reached for another to try again.

"That's not what I meant, idiot," she said. She turned to their mother to see if she understood and saw that she was looking away, across the lake. The girl looked that way too, and saw the smoke rising from the far shore. All they could make out was an untended small fire; there was no person to be seen.

"What's that?" asked the girl. "A campfire? Is someone over there?"

The pilot had gotten out of the float plane. He was a young man with a full red beard who wore rubber hip boots so he could walk in the water to a small door in the back of the plane that opened up the baggage compartment. Carrying the first of their duffel bags, he set it down on the dry grass at the edge of the beach and started back to get another. He saw that the girl and her mother were looking intently across the lake and he looked for himself. He could see no one there, either.

"Don't worry about that, ma'am," he dismissed. "That'll just be a Qualik. He won't bother you folks with what you're here to do."

The boy stopped throwing rocks and turned to see what they were talking about. "What's a Qualik?" he asked.

"An Indian, stupid," answered his sister. "It was in the book Mom gave us. Didn't you even look at it?"

"Hey, hey," said the mother gently. "Remember why we're here, okay?"

Admonished, the two children grew quiet. The pilot finished carrying their gear to the beach, and then he approached the woman. There was deference — and some concern that he couldn't hide — in his eyes. He looked at the package, and then at the woman and her two children.

"Are you sure you want to do this, ma'am?" he asked. "I know you and the kids are experienced, but this place is pretty isolated. It's no problem for me to take you right back to Port Nerka, and you could be in Anchorage tomorrow morning."

The children looked at their mother. Her eyes were clear, and there was no anxiety in them.

"Thank you, but no," she smiled at the pilot. "This is something we have to do, and we have to do it here."

"Then at least let me set up your tent, help you get arranged . . ."

"Thanks again, really, but no," answered the woman. "That too is something we have to do as a family. And we sure do know how to set up our camp, don't we, kids?"

"Yeah," answered the boy enthusiastically. "And my mom knows how to find the North Star."

"It's not that hard, dummy," dismissed his sister, rolling her eyes. Then to the pilot she said, "My dad usually comes, too, but he said we could handle this on our own, right, Mom?"

The woman smiled awkwardly at the pilot, slightly embarrassed by the family details coming out in the open. This was the only family trip any of them had ever made without all four being together, and the night before the three had left home the woman and her husband had taken their children out into their back yard and shown them the North Star.

A Fable of Salmon, Northern Lights and an Old Promise Kept

"See, kids?" the woman had said. "Daddy can see the North Star from right here, and we'll be able to see it from all the way up in Alaska at the same time. It will help to keep us closer while we're gone."

"Where is it, Mom?" the boy had worried. "I can't see which one. I need to see which one!"

And so the woman had shown her son how to find the North Star, gently holding his hand and tracing with his finger the imaginary line running from the Big Dipper to Polaris and whispering as she hugged him that tomorrow they were going to be a little bit closer to the only star in the night sky that doesn't ever move.

Remembering that moment, she put her arms around her son and squeezed him. But here on the beach with the bush pilot the woman did not want to let the discussion trend any further in the direction it was headed. The North Star was a private family matter, not a navigational tool: Among her carefully selected equipment for this trip was a portable GPS receiver that she knew how to use. She looked at the pilot as she held her son.

"Do you have children?" she asked.

"Yes, ma'am," he answered. "I've got three at home in Port Nerka."

The woman nodded. "It's an important part of any trip with kids, don't you think, to let them set up their own gear?"

The pilot looked at the children, then again at the woman. "Well, ma'am" he said, "I do respect what you're here for and I guess I'll leave you alone to do it. You can count on seeing me here ten days from today, unless you call on the radio sooner." The pilot touched his hat and turned toward his airplane.

"It will be sooner, don't you think?" asked the woman to his retreating back. He turned around.

"I hope it won't be ten days," continued the woman. "I have physics classes at the university to teach and they start next week. Do you really think it will be that long?"

The pilot looked at the lake, gauged its depth and thought about the temperature of the water. "It might. Water's still a touch high. Then again, you might see them tomorrow." He started back toward the plane, then stopped again.

"Remember now," he said. "Six in the morning, noon, six at night. That's when we monitor the radio. If we don't hear from you for forty-eight hours, I'm coming back immediately." The pilot hesitated, to make sure the woman understood.

"We'll be fine," the woman said firmly. "We really will."

The pilot took a long breath. "Ma'am, I don't doubt it. But please, don't go the forty-eight hours unless you absolutely have to."

The woman smiled at him. "No. No, we won't."

This time the pilot did leave. Grasping both blades of the airplane's propeller, he pushed the plane out into the water until it floated free, then he leaned against a pontoon so that the airplane began to swing around, pointing its nose out toward the center of the lake. He hopped up onto a pontoon and climbed into the cockpit and turned the ignition key. The engine popped once, twice, and then roared alive. Blown wind and a fine, wet spray billowed behind the airplane as it accelerated across the water, gaining speed and skimming lightly on the surface until the pilot rocked the wings slightly to break the surface tension so he could lift one pontoon, and then the other, from the lake's surface. Swiftly the little airplane climbed up and away, back in the direction it had come from, its engine steadily droning and growing quieter, reversing the sound it had made when it had first appeared.

The family of three stood silently on their small beach at the edge of the green lake and watched the airplane go away until there was neither sight nor sound to indicate that it had ever been there. Once again the felt quietude of wilderness descended on each of them.

The woman, despite the calm self-assurance that she had been careful to demonstrate to the bush pilot, wasn't without reservations about being here.

How could she be, with her children here too? It was true that she had camped in wilderness places since she had been a very young girl, and she had made certain that her own children were comfortable and capable in the outdoors. But this was on every level she could imagine a very distant place, and it now seemed to be moving on its own, traveling even farther away, as if the tiny disappearing airplane and the concerned pilot were frozen in place, locked in their own space and time while the green lake itself accelerated away toward the unknown, taking the family of three with it. Feeling the onset of an involuntary shudder, the woman quickly put the package on the ground and reached out and pulled her children close, warding off the psychic chill as she hugged them by their shoulders.

Well, she thought as she looked down at the quiet package, we're here now, aren't we? And it isn't as if we had a choice, is it?

They stood that way without speaking for a long time before the woman let go and looked again at the small, carefully wrapped package while the children watched. Neither of them knew what to say; they knew what was in it. The woman reached down to pick the package up and as she did, the beartooth amulet slipped out from under her shirt and dangled lightly on the thong that held it around her neck. In the shape of a leaping salmon, the two-inch-long amulet had years ago lost its bright ivory brilliance to the subtle shadings of tan and brown that now highlighted what had once been delicately etched fins, scales and gill plates. The bright midday sun caught on the tiny salmon's flashing eye, an inlay of cobalt-blue Northern abalone shell so rich with depth and color that it seemed to magnify the sun's rays that struck it, separating the light into a vivid, shifting spectrum that seemed to send out more light than it took in.

"Wow, Mom," breathed the girl. "I never saw you wear that before."

"It was your great-grandmother's," answered the woman to her daughter. She held the amulet for a moment longer in the sunlight, and then she carefully placed it back inside her shirt, its soothing coolness resting against her skin while she cradled the package in her arms. The children watched and waited, but she didn't say anything more. Finally the boy spoke:

"You loved Great Gramma a lot, didn't you, Mom?" he said.

"I still do," the woman answered. "The love doesn't go away just because someone dies. Sometimes it grows even stronger."

"Did it with you and Great Gramma?" asked the girl.

The woman looked down at the package of ashes she so softly held. "I don't know, darling," she answered. "I've loved her so much, for so long, ever since I was a little girl, it doesn't even seem to me that she's gone yet. I'm not ready to let go of her. I'm really not."

The children looked up to see that their mother's eyes had filled with tears, and they both reached around to hug her with wet eyes of their own. They both had loved their great-grandmother, too, even though they hadn't seen much of her in the recent past. The children knew that their mother was the old woman's only grandchild, making them her only great-grandchildren. But they also knew that there was a deeper and much more private bond between the two women, one that had existed since their mother was a young girl and had spent her summers with her grandmother, camping and sailing and learning to love wild things and faraway places. Since then the two women had been inseparable. "She's my best friend," their mother would say without trying to explain any further. "And she always has been."

It had been the only thing that their mother and father had ever argued about, once so badly that it had been the only time either of the children had ever seen their mother leave the house in tears. The children never heard enough of the rare arguments to understand what they were about, and, anyway, they had ended some time ago, about the time that their great-grandmother had gotten so infirm that she could no longer come and visit. After that, their mother used to telephone her grandmother on Sunday nights, sometimes talking for an hour or more, and the tension seemed to go out of the household. As far as the children could tell, anyway.

"Why did Great Gramma pick this lake?" the boy asked, not taking his eyes off the package. "Did she used to come here?"

"She told me she came here just once," the woman answered. "But this is the lake she wanted. Most certainly this is the lake."

"Why?" asked the boy.

His mother's eyes traveled back across the lake to rest again on the campfire on the far shore. "She wouldn't say. She told me how to get to the lake, and she told me when to spread her ashes. But she wouldn't say why. That, she said, we had to learn for ourselves once we got here."

"Have you and Dad been here, Mom?" asked the boy.

"No, darling," she answered. "Neither one of us has been to this lake, or even to this part of Alaska before. We'll have to tell him all about it when we get home."

"How come he didn't come?" asked the boy. "He always does."

The woman hesitated before answering, even though she knew she should not; she knew how acutely sensitive the children were, especially her daughter, to any conflict, however temporary or minor, between their parents. But the truth was that her husband could have come, but he had chosen not to. He hadn't wanted her and the children to make this trip at all, even though he knew how little choice she had, and they had quietly argued over it without agreement right up until the morning she and the children had left for Alaska. In all their time together, neither she nor her husband had ever gone away from the other with any cloud, let alone one as dark as this, hanging between them. Desperately the woman wanted this trip to be over. But it wasn't, and now she was here, irrevocably and with no control over when it would end. The pilot's offer to take them right back to Port Nerka had been more tempting than she wanted to admit openly to herself, even if she knew how impossible it was to accept.

"How come?" insisted the boy. "How come Dad didn't come with us?" The woman took a breath as she reinstalled her resolve. It was something she was very good at.

"Because this isn't a vacation, just like we told you before, darling," she answered to her son. "This is a promise that I made to Great Gramma, so it's something that I have to do alone, not with Daddy."

"Then how come we're here," asked the girl.

"Because that's what your great-grandmother wanted," answered the woman. She looked at each of her children. "Bringing you two with me was the most important part of the promise. It's what she wanted the most."

More than wanted, the woman then said only to herself. Demanded. Insisting with an intensity that her grandmother had only shown that one time in her very long life, demanding as the final call of a lifelong love and with the force of morality itself, that her only granddaughter bring her ashes to this place, to this unnamed green lake at precisely this time of the year, and — most important of all — that she bring the two children when she did. Now the younger woman had done precisely that, fulfilling a requirement that she did not yet understand and at a price to be paid later at home in a currency that the woman wasn't sure she would have when she got there. How would she be able to explain this journey to her husband until she fully understood it herself? If she ever did.

But it was done, or at least started. She and her children were here, and they would deal with it. That, at least, they knew how to do. The woman turned and walked to the top of the beach and gently set the package down, upright on a soft tuft of green grass.

"Okay," she said to the children. "Let's carry the gear up here. It looks like a good, dry spot. It's time to pitch the tent and make camp."

A Fable of Salmon, Northern Lights and an Old Promise Kept

The girl turned and walked toward the duffels, but the boy held back. "When?" he asked.

"Now, of course," answered his mother. "Before it gets dark."

"No," he said. "I meant when do we put Great Gramma's ashes on the lake?"

"Oh," his mother said gently. "I'm sorry. I thought you knew." She put her arm around his thin shoulders, pulled him close against her as together they looked out at the green water of the lake.

"We're waiting for something to happen, darling," she told her son. "For something that happens every year at this same place and this same time. A thing that your great-grandmother thought was the most important thing in the whole world. We're waiting for the sockeye salmon to return to this lake, the very same lake where every one of them was born."

The ocean water in which the sockeye swam, always dark, grew even darker as she approached the coast, homing in with all the other salmon in her pod toward the mouth of the river where every one of them had been born, and from which every one of them had descended to the sea. The atmosphere above the water here was a tumult of weather in conflict: Warming ocean winds wafted toward shore to meet colder mountain downdrafts tumbling like invisible waterfalls from the high snowfields, roiling together into the shifting confusion of squalling winds, rainfall and thickening fog that was an almost permanent condition along this wild, uninhabited shore. The sun's direct light, so common out at sea, rarely struck the water here along the coast, and the sockeye found themselves swimming in strange water that seemed to lose its light as it grew shallower.

Tendrils of fresh water began to weave through the pod of salmon and its effect on the massed fish was electric, stimulating, immediate and universal. The swimming salmon sensed the one message it carried identically to each of them, and they turned as a unit toward the source of the sweetwater tendrils, drawn by a nameless convergence of every molecule in each of their bodies.

And so they came, a closing path arcing smoothly toward the point of its own beginning. Directed by a certainty immune to question and drawn by a knowledge undiluted by thought, the salmon swam into the estuary where the river of their birth flowed into the ocean of their lives.

Tell us about Great Gramma," asked the boy. "Tell us about when she lived here."

It was evening, on the first day of their trip to the green lake. On the soft grass behind the beach they had set up two lightweight tents, one for the woman and the other for the boy and girl. They had gathered dried sticks for a campfire, and it now burned brightly on the gravel beach, near to the water and safely away from the forest behind the tents. The three family members sat around the fire and watched its glowing embers rise in a dissipating heat plume toward the stars above.

"Your great-grandmother was born here in Alaska," said the woman. "In Port Nerka, just before the turn of this century."

"A hundred years ago," said the girl.

"A hundred years, that's right," smiled her mother. "She lived a very long life. And the first part of it was up here, out among all the islands and settlements of the North Coast people."

"The Indians," said the boy, making a face at his sister.

"Yes, but they call themselves Qualiks, and you should too. To your great-grandmother they were always the North Coast people when she talked about them."

"She was a teacher, wasn't she, Mom?" said the girl. "Just like you."

"She was a teacher, but not in a university like me. She taught arithmetic to kids more your age, in what they called grammar school. When she was here in Alaska, though, she was a young woman and she only worked in a missionary school for a short time before she moved away and married your great-grandfather. She never came back, even though she loved this place more than any other in the whole world."

"Why not?" asked the girl.

The woman looked at her daughter. "I don't know," she said as her hand lifted almost involuntarily to the amulet lying quietly under her shirt. "It was the only thing she never would talk about."

The girl watched her mother's hand. "Did Great Gramma get . . . that when she lived here?"

"Yes she did," answered the woman. "It's a Qualik amulet, and she wore it all the time."

"What's an amulet?" asked the boy.

"It's jewelry, can't you see?" said the girl. "It's for good luck, right, Mom?"

"Something like that," smiled her mother. "The Qualik people made them for each other to help keep away bad spirits and other troubles."

"You mean it's magic?" said the boy, his eyes going wider. "What can it do?" His sister rolled her eyes.

"No, stupid," she derided. "Mom doesn't believe in that kind of magic and neither should you."

"Great Gramma did," insisted the boy. "She told me."

"I know she did, darling," soothed his mother, running her hand through the boy's hair. "But Great Gramma loved magic stories, like the ones she used to tell us. She didn't believe magic happened in real life."

"I think she did," pouted the boy. "Just like she said."

The woman and the girl both said nothing. They knew the boy's moods, and they knew there was no point in pursuing the point any further. In his own good time he would come to understand, but it would be something he would want to do on his own, without being pushed into it.

"How come Great Gramma wanted us to bring her ashes here, Mom?" asked the girl, changing the subject.

"To wait for the salmon," interjected her brother. "Mom already told you that."

"Yeah, but how did she know they would come?"

"The salmon come every year at the same time, darling," answered the woman to her daughter. "They swim up the river from the ocean and they lay their eggs in this lake, or in the little brooks that flow into it. Then, when the eggs are hatched, the young salmon live in this lake for a couple of years until they are big enough to swim down the river and into the ocean where they live together for the rest of their lives. Then one day, years later, they all swim together back to this very same lake where they were born, so that they can lay their own eggs in exactly the same spot where each of them was born. That's the life cycle of the sockeye salmon, just like the other four species of Pacific salmon. They always return to the place where they were born. Your great-grandmother knew all about that because she grew up here."

"How do the salmon know how to do that, Mom?" asked the girl. "How do they find their way back?"

"No one really knows, darling," answered her mother. "There are a lot of theories, but it's a natural process that remains a mystery to modern science. All we know is that they do, every generation of salmon, every year, to the precise place where they were born, and always at the same time."

The boy was quiet, looking at the lake and wanting to stay angry, but the explanation had captured his interest. "Then what, Mom?" he finally asked. "Do the salmon swim back to the ocean, or do they stay here?"

His mother turned to him, and then she moved closer to her young son. She put her arm around the boy and lightly hugged him. "After they lay their eggs, darling," she said gently, "they die. They've reproduced themselves and now their lives are complete. They have to make room for the next generation of salmon, the ones still in their eggs."

"All of them die?" asked the boy. "Right here in this lake?"

"All of them, yes," answered the woman. "When they come back here, it means it's the end of of their lives."

The girl walked over and joined the other two. For a long moment the family was quiet, as quiet as the lake that lay before them. The boy picked up a small pebble and tossed it underhand out toward the water; it arced and splashed lightly before wobbling to rest on the bottom, disappearing among all the others.

"Just like Great Gramma," said the boy.

The river itself still lay before her, somewhere very near as she swam in the saltwater estuary, but now the sockeye knew it was there. All her life this one salmon had done nothing other than simply react to the instantly compiled sum of what her senses detected and her instincts dictated, and this set of automatic processes did not change now. That this was to be the dramatic culmination of her entire existence meant nothing, absolutely nothing, to the fish as she swam with thousands of her biological replicates, circling the shallow estuary and tasting the intermixed outflows of fresh water that came intermittently from somewhere, somewhere. Somewhere.

Turning in unison, swimming with a directed singularity as if they were one entity, the thousands of salmon circled the bay together, a mass of fully wound biological coilsprings waiting for the cosmic tick that would release each of them into their final headlong dash against the arrow of time.

In the morning the family awoke early, and the woman sent her children down the beach to gather more driftwood for the day's fire. The boy scampered ahead, ignoring all the sticks that lay on the beach and instead searching for flat stones to toss out onto the water, trying to skip them. His sister lagged behind him, carefully selecting individual pieces of firewood. She hadn't expected much help from her brother, but she didn't really mind that he provided none at all. In fact she was happy to choose and gather all the wood; she preferred picking things out for herself. And besides, it was fun. When she had an armful, she turned back toward the campsite where their mother had started a breakfast fire with the last of the previous night's wood.

A shadow dipped across the stones in front of the girl and she looked up to see a lone raven flying above. *Cr-r-uck!* called the raven as it winged out and over the lake, flying toward the far shore. It was the first bird the girl had seen on this trip and she stopped to watch it.

"Hey, look!" called out her brother behind her.

The girl turned and saw that he was pointing out over the water. At first she thought that he was pointing to the raven as it flew, but then she saw what had caught his eye. Smoke once again rose from the campfire across the lake. Her brother ran back to be beside her and together they looked over there as the flying raven reached the other side. Backing its wings to slow down, the large black bird settled in a tall spruce near the distant campfire.

A human figure appeared beside the campfire, slowly walking. It was so far away that the children couldn't see it well, but they could tell it was a man, that he seemed to be an old man, and they could see that he was wearing around his shoulders a dark blanket that reached the ground. As they watched, the old man squatted down by his fire across the lake.

Together the children ran back to their own camp to tell their mother.

"Mom! Mom! Look! Look!" they shouted, pointing as they ran.

"What is it?" called their mother, alarmed. Seeing where they pointed, she peered that way herself, holding her hand across her eyes as she tried to make out what they had seen. The breathless children came up beside her.

"See? See?" the boy exclaimed. "It's the Indian! It's the Indian the pilot said!"

"The Qualik," said his sister. "Mom said not to call him an Indian."

Their mother stared hard at where they pointed. "I don't see anyone," she said. "Just the campfire over there."

The squatting figure of the old man was still there and the boy and the girl could see him clearly.

"He's right there, Mom! Right beside his fire. Can't you see him?" they pleaded.

"No," the woman answered. "I can't. I just see the rock beside the fire."

The girl ran to one of the tents and grabbed her mother's binoculars, then ran back and handed them to her. "Here!" she said in exasperation. "See?"

The woman brought the binoculars to her eyes and focused them. Very carefully she scanned the far shore. Then she brought down the binoculars and handed them back to her daughter. "There's no one there," she said patiently. "It's just your imagination."

The boy grabbed for the binoculars but his sister yanked them out of his reach before he could get them. "Wait," she hissed in annoyance as she lifted them to look for herself. She trained the binoculars in the right direction and turned the focus knob to match her own eyes. The campfire came into sharp relief and right beside it was . . .

A large, dark rock. A boulder the same size as a squatting-down person, right where the man had been. Frantically she scanned the shore. No one was there. She turned the binoculars to the tall spruce. The raven was gone, too.

"No!" she exclaimed. "It was a man! It was! We saw him!"

Her brother snatched the binoculars and looked. When he saw that it was just a boulder, he began to cry. "No-o-o-oh-oh-oh!" he wailed. "What did you do, Mom? Why did you make him go away?! It was an Indian. We saw an Indian!"

"Oh no, darling," his mother soothed. "I didn't make anything go away. You just made a mistake. You just let your imagination run away, that's all."

"It was an Indian and you made him go away!" pouted the boy. He glared at his mother, then turned to look again at the campfire across the lake. "Come back, Indian!" he shouted. "Please come back!"

His mother put her arm around his shoulders and tried to pull him close to her but the boy wrenched himself away.

"It was an *Indian*," he said with his jaw clenched. "And you didn't want him to be, and now he's gone." The boy turned and stalked away, toward the trees behind the two tents. His mother started to follow him, but then she thought better of it and decided to let him go.

The girl came up beside her mother and together they watched the boy sit down beside a spruce tree, sulking.

"It was a man, Mom," the girl said. "It really was. It was an old Qualik man sitting beside the fire, and then when you looked, it was a rock, right in the same place."

The woman put her arm around her daughter and laughed. "I hope not, angel," she said. "My physics students are going to have a tough semester if I've turned into Medusa."

The woman looked again across the lake. There really was nothing there; no sign of an old man or any other person. Just the empty beach, the hills behind and the lake in front, calmly reflecting the blue sky above and a distant white whisp of mare's tails above the western horizon.

Rain, she thought. Probably by tonight.

t grew darker for the gathered pod of salmon, still waiting in saltwater. Overhead, the surface of the bay was tossed by slashing gusts of wind, was pattered and pitted by blown droplets of rain. Beneath the passing storm, the pod of salmon milled in confusion, each individual fish for the first time in its life not fleeing toward the serenity of deeper water, for there was none to dive into. Nor did the salmon turn and run out to sea, for they could not. Wracked by an internal conflict none of them had ever felt, the salmon stayed in the shallow, storm-tossed bay, their individual survival instincts overridden by a collective drive that was now stronger than anything that had yet been triggered inside any of them singly.

And so, driven more to stay than to flee, the salmon swam in excited, undirected circles. Around and around the small estuary they swam, staying close to the shore, buffeted by storm surf and tide surge, tightly bound together by identical sets of reactions and waiting in an absence of wonder for something to happen.

Miles inland from the salmon, far upstream in the valley of the river that had called them back, rain fell. Great downpours of opened clouds that ran down, across and over the land, gathering in trickles that flowed into rushes, swelling to rivulets and running unchecked into the river itself. A lifting surge of living fresh water gathered in the high country and poured itself downhill, running the length of the river and coursing with strength and speed toward the coastal estuary, toward the open ocean. Toward all the waiting sockeye salmon.

Together the mother and daughter made breakfast. The gathering rain clouds now rose higher in the western sky as the girl kept looking toward the far shore, at where she had seen the old man, but nothing over there changed. Where the man had been was a dark rock, just as her mother had said. When it was almost time to serve the breakfast they had made, the woman told the girl to go and fetch her brother so he could eat. She stood up to do it, and saw that her brother was no longer beside the spruce tree where he had been sitting and sulking. With her hands on her hips, the girl looked around, and then she saw him.

"He's gone down the beach, Mom," she said.

"Well, you better go get him," the woman answered. "He needs his breakfast."

Down the beach, the boy was walking determinedly, not stopping for any skipping stones and heading away from their camp. Far behind, he heard the voice of his sister calling him to breakfast. He turned to look and when he saw her coming, he began to run. He didn't want breakfast, he wanted to find the old man.

The boy ran along the beach around the edge of the lake, and his sister ran after him. He ran until he was out of breath and then he walked, with his sister catching up and calling to him. Still he kept going until he was almost to where the old man had been, and then he stopped.

There was no old man. And now there was no rock, either. There was nothing. Where the fire had been there wasn't an ember; there wasn't even a blackened fire ring. There was just gravel and dried sticks, just like every other part of the beach around the green lake.

The boy stood in amazement as his sister caught up to him, completely out of breath. She was angry and about to grab him when she noticed what he had already seen. That there was nothing there.

Together they looked around, and then they looked at each other with wide eyes. "Maybe we're not in the right spot," said the girl.

A shadow passed over them, just like the one that had passed in front of the girl earlier, and the two children looked up. A raven again, flying higher overhead and going away from the lake. *Cr-r-uck*, it called, softer than before.

They looked again around them and this time they spotted a small stream flowing into the lake just beyond where they stood. "I didn't see that before," said the boy.

Together they walked to the stream and stopped beside it. The water that flowed from it into the green lake was so clear that all they could see was the sparkling light reflected from its tumbling surface as it purled over the pebbles and rocks of the small channel it had formed on its way through the beach into the lake. As they looked into the stream water, the two children saw fish swimming in it, pointed upstream. They were tiny, like miniature trout and there were hundreds of them, none more than an inch long.

"Are those the salmon?" breathed the boy.

"No, dummy," said his sister. "Salmon are big. These are minnows."

"Maybe they're babies," said the boy.

"Maybe," said his sister. "Mom will know. Let's go get her." She started back toward their camp, walked several steps and then noticed that her brother wasn't with her. She turned back, annoyed again, and she saw that he was staring at something she couldn't see, something just out of her sight upstream in the little creek. She went back to him.

It was the old man. Definitely a Qualik man, wrapped in the dark blanket they had seen him in before. He was standing on a rock, bent over next to a deeper part of the little creek, and he was concentrating so hard on something in the water that he seemed not to have noticed the children nearby. The boy started to walk toward him and the girl rushed over and grabbed her brother's arm.

"No-oh," she whispered. "Let's go."

A Fable of Salmon, Northern Lights and an Old Promise Kept

"Uh uh," answered her brother. He pulled his arm free and walked quietly toward the old man. Closer and closer he approached as his apprehensive sister watched, not daring to speak. Closer and closer . . .

"Sh-h-h-h," said the old man without moving. "You are making too much noise."

The boy stopped. He was just a few feet behind the old man, but he couldn't see what the old man was looking at in the water. "We thought you were an Indian," said the boy, speaking softly.

Slowly, the old man turned to face the boy. "And why do you now think I am not?" he asked, looking the boy sternly in the eyes. "What do you think I am instead?"

The boy's eyes grew wide in fear, and he stepped back, tripped on a rock, and scrambled to his feet.

"He meant to say 'Qualik,' mister," said the girl. "He didn't mean 'Indian'."

The old man turned and looked slowly at the girl without changing his expression. She was frightened, but she didn't run. Turning to her brother, she urged him with her eyes to come toward her so they could get away from here. "He's real sorry, mister," she said to the old man. "He really is. He didn't mean anything."

"The boy spoke it, so he meant to say it." The old man turned to look once again at the boy. "If what you know is true, never be sorry for telling it."

The old man turned back to the stream and resumed what he had been doing, staring intently into the water. The boy and the girl looked at each other, and the girl urged her brother with her eyes to leave, to go back to the safety of their own camp. The boy shook his head. Once again he stepped closer to see what the old man was doing.

"What are you doing?" asked the boy.

The old man didn't turn around. "The same as you," he answered as he concentrated on the water. "Waiting for nerka."

THE LAKE OF THE BEGINNING

44

"What's a nerka?"

The old man didn't answer. The stream before him gurgled and ran. It was deeper in this spot, and the bottom was hard to see, a mix of deep blue and rich greens shifting and out of focus through the swiftly flowing water. The boy turned to his sister and saw a look of sudden understanding come across her face.

"It's the sockeye," she exclaimed. "Nerka means sockeye salmon. I knew that."

"That's what we're doing," said the boy. "We're waiting for the salmon, too."

"I know," said the old man, still focused on the water under his gaze.

"How did you know that?" asked the boy.

The old man didn't answer. Instead, his body tightened under the dark blanket that covered it and he sank to his knees. Then very slowly he leaned out over the water, farther and farther with just his knees on the streamside rock, until it seemed that he had to fall into the water, he was leaning so far out and over the surface. Like the flashing strike of a heron's beak, his arm shot out from under the blanket and instantly down into the water. Splash!

The old man pulled back his arm from the water, and in his grasp came a rainbow trout, writhing and struggling in the old man's iron grip. Quickly and painlessly the old man killed the trout, then sat back on his haunches, gathered the blanket over his shoulders, and stood up. The fish was still in his hand.

"Why did you do that?" exclaimed the girl.

"For my breakfast," answered the old man. "Even an Indian has to eat." For the first time since they had seen him, a twinkle of amusement showed in the old man's eyes.

"Can we have some?" asked the boy. "We didn't have any breakfast."

"Of course you can," said the old man as he started walking toward the lake shore. "There are plenty more in the stream. Get one for yourself while I make a fire."

The boy looked hungrily at the fish, then at his sister. He scampered toward the rock where the old man had caught the trout. The girl came up beside her brother and looked into the water. She shook her head and then turned toward the old man as he walked away with his fish.

"We can't see anything," she called to him. "We can't see into the water. There's too much glare."

"Then look harder," he said without turning.

"I can see," said the boy. "I can see right to the bottom."

"No you can't," sneered the girl. "That's the reflection on top. You can't see past it."

"Yes I can," he insisted. "I see a trout."

"Oh, right," she said. "Are you sure it isn't a whale?"

The boy didn't answer. Trying to copy what he had seen the old man do, he tensed his small body and leaned out over the water, staring into it.

"You're going to get wet," said his sister.

The boy coiled his legs, pointed his hand at the water, and sprung straight into it. Ker-splash! Water shot out in all directions, soaking the girl. "He-ey!" she yelled, turning away. "You jerk! Lookit!"

The old man stopped and looked back. The girl moved away from the stream and tried to brush the water off her clothes, face and arms. It was cold. "You big jerk!" she said. "I'm all wet! Lookit!"

But her brother didn't answer. Still face down in the water, he seemed intent on getting his imagined trout. The current of the stream carried him down toward the lake, and still he didn't look up. He didn't move at all. Angry at him, his sister started toward the stream.

"No!" cried their mother. She had just appeared from the gravel beach, and when she saw her son face down in the stream, she sprinted to him. Splashing into the waist-deep flow, she grabbed the limp body of the little boy, lifted his head from the water and pulled him out and to dry land. Blood streamed from an open gash on his forehead.

"Oh no. Oh no. Oh no," moaned the woman as she set the boy down on the grass beside the stream. She put her head down, right next to his with her ear against his mouth, listening — praying — to hear his breathing, and just as she did this, the boy coughed. Water shot from his mouth. He coughed again, and his mother reached under his shoulders and lifted him to a sitting position. He coughed, over and over, racking, wet coughs that expelled the water from his lungs as he took in sobbing gasps of fresh air between them. When his breathing seemed calmer and assured, his mother took a cloth from her pocket and pressed it to the cut on his forehead. Holding it there, she took the boy in her arms and cradled him, rocking back and forth, holding him to her breast with her eyes closed against the tears that filled them, her whole body shivering uncontrollably from the frozen fear that still had not left her.

"Thank God," she whispered. "Oh, thank God."

The girl had been locked in place across the stream the whole time, and now she came across, oblivious to the cold water as she walked through it and over to her mother and brother.

"Mom, I didn't . . ." she said in a whisper, barely able to get it out. "He just jumped in. I didn't . . ."

Keeping one arm around the boy to hold the makeshift bandage in place, the woman reached out to her daughter, and the girl came down on the rocks, reaching around her mother and brother as she broke out in uncontrolled tears. The boy began to cry, too.

"It's okay, darlings," the woman said, pulling them close as the tears welled in her own eyes. "It's okay. Everything's okay now. We're going to be fine." The three of them sat there together, shaking, wet, crying and hugging each other.

The woman looked up at the old Qualik man who had made no move to save her son as he lay face down in the water, drowning. Waves of fear, relief and rage rolled and broke through her as she stared at him with pleading eyes.

"Why?" she sobbed, her voice quavering. "Why didn't you do something? Why didn't you do something? He was drowning!"

Across the stream, the old man stood watching impassively. He said nothing, showed no sign of remorse or embarrassment or relief that the boy was all right. As he watched the three distraught family members huddled together on the ground across the stream from him, he showed no sign of anything at all.

The woman couldn't bear any longer to look at him, and she turned back to her children, hugging them even tighter as she cried, trying to envelop them entirely, blanketing them as if her arms were wings folded without seams around them.

Gradually as she held them the cold shivering of the children slowed; the heat from their warming bodies worked through the wet clothes they wore and radiated steadily into the woman herself. The rigidity left her shoulders and melted away from her back; her arms grew heavy and a languor spread through her whole being, like oncoming sleep. She felt herself wanting to stay there for-ever, wrapped around her warming children as they breathed quietly in her arms. For a moment she gave herself over to it. And then she looked up.

The old man was gone.

The woman stood unsteadily and helped her children to their feet. Then she turned away from where the old man had been, and, on shaking legs almost too weak to do it, started walking away with her arms around her two children, around the green lake, all the way back to their own side.

At the mouth of the river, in the estuary where she swam with all the other thousands of her kind, it was dark. But the absence of light meant nothing to the sockeye, for she had spent most of her life deep within it. Darkness, even as it approached absolute black, was neither good nor bad, neither dangerous nor benign, neither comforting nor sinister; light simply was or was not present.

Tonight it was not. Under a thickness of clouds that blocked every possible glimmer of starlight and moonshine, a great surge of fresh water that had been fed by fast-moving inland storms came roiling out of the mountains, cascading down the river and tumbling into the estuary. The salmon felt it almost instantly.

Turning together like silver shards of living metal suddenly drawn by a magnet, the salmon — all the salmon, each and every sockeye salmon in the unlit waters of the bay — pivoted toward the river. Deep in the compacted pod of accelerating fish, the lone sockeye went with them all as surely as they went with her, caught up in an impulse of regeneration and surging with collected strength and complete abandon against the growing flood that had now, finally, called.

It was night now in the camp of the family and it was raining. The three sat together under a waterproof nylon tarpaulin stretched over a pair of spruce poles and pegged into the grassy ground behind them. In the front of this slim but effective shelter they had built a small fire, setting it just under the outermost edge of the tarp to keep the rain from striking it directly but close enough to the open air so that the smoke blew out and away, disappearing in the swirling night wind into the sodden, pitch-dark air above.

The woman had wrapped a clean, white gauze bandage around her son's head. He had a headache, but in all other respects he seemed not to have been hurt badly. The bleeding had long since ceased, his eyes were clear and he wasn't sleepy. In fact, as the wind and rain splatted on the tarp, sending mists of dampness occasionally under it and onto the three people there, causing his mother and sister to huddle closer together and pull their collars tight around their necks, the boy was happily roasting a marshmallow.

"Will this storm make the salmon stay away?" asked the girl, turning to her mother.

"I don't know, darling," she answered. "But I doubt it. The salmon have to swim up a river to get here, and rain puts more water in the river. I bet it helps them get here sooner."

"I hope so," said the boy.

"Me too," echoed the girl.

"Me three," said their mother. The children both looked at her. It was an old family joke that was usually said by one of them. Their mother smiled.

"I do think they will," she said. "Remember, the salmon come back to spawn at the same time every year, and this is the week Great Gramma said they would be here."

Outside the ring of light from the family's campfire, the wind gusted. Trees moaned and cracked in the darkened forest behind them, and a blown spatter of harder rain crackled on the whipping tarp above their heads. But they had fixed the shelter well, placing rocks and a small but heavy tree trunk at the back of the tarp where it lay on the ground; it was anchored there and no wind or rain could get under it. Out on the lake in front of them, unseeable in the dark night, waves ran irregularly across the surface and broke against the shoreline rocks.

"Mom," asked the boy, "can I give the Indian man a marshmallow?"

"Don't be silly," answered the woman. "It's nighttime and its storming. And I don't want you going over there again even in the daylight. It's too far away, and I don't think we'll see that old man again anyway. I don't think he's all —"

"Mom . . ." said the girl.

"I mean it," said the woman.

"Mom," insisted the girl. "He's here."

The woman looked up sharply, and saw where her two children were staring. There on the beach, at the edge of the light from their fire and standing silent and upright with the rain drenching down on him, was the old Qualik man. His dark blanket was drawn close over his shoulders and held tight around his neck, but he had on no hat. His long black hair, streaked with gray, hung straight down from his head, soaking wet and matted down over his shoulders. He was as still as a tree stump in the dark and his eyes reflected the dancing firelight as he stood watching them. He made no move to come into the shelter of their tarpaulin, even after they had finally noticed that he was there.

"What do you want?" called the woman to him, but the old man did not answer, did not move. The rain continued; the wind rose and fell. The old man stood without moving in the swirling storm, watching them without blinking as the water ran continuously down his ancient face.

"Oh, don't just stand there, then," said the woman to him. "Come in out of the rain."

The old man stepped forward, ducked his head at the edge of the tarpaulin and came in under it. The boy and the girl moved around the campfire toward their mother, making room for him to sit down. He did.

"Thank you," said the old man.

"Are you all right?" asked the woman.

"Yes," said the old man.

"Do you need anything?" she asked.

"No," said the old man.

For a long minute, no one spoke. The family members waited to see what he would say, but he said nothing. Steam rose from his blanket as the warmth of the fire touched it. The girl looked to her mother.

"Do you want a marshmallow?" asked the boy. The old man looked at him, and the boy reached out with the green stick he held. On the end of it was a toasted marshmallow, burned to black on one side and smoking.

"Thank you," said the old man. He reached out from under his dark blanket and took the stick with the marshmallow from the boy. With his other hand he pulled the melted, sticky mass of sugar from the stick, carefully separated it into two globs and put one of them into his mouth. He chewed it carefully without expression, swallowed it and handed the stick back to the boy. Then he tossed the other glob of marshmallow into the fire.

"What's the matter?" asked the boy. "Didn't you like it?"

"It was delicious," answered the old man.

"Then why did you throw the rest away?"

"I didn't throw it away," said the old man. "Because it was good, I shared it."

"With the fire?" asked the girl. "You shared a marshmallow with the fire?"

The old man didn't answer. Instead he turned to the woman, and waited. She looked back at him and realized that he expected her to give an answer, just the way her grandmother used to do in order to coax an answer from her when the woman was a girl. No one had done that to her in years. But she did know the answer; her grandmother had always told stories about the North Coast people and this was one that she knew. Keeping her eyes on the old man, she spoke:

"The Qualik people believe that living persons have a responsibility for the spirits of those who have already died. They believe that they must share some of their food with the spirits of their dead relatives, because the spirits no longer have bodies on earth and can no longer get their own food. That's why he threw a bit of the marshmallow into the fire, so the food could follow his ancestors into the next world where they all have gone."

In the old man's eyes the firelight flickered brighter. The deep creases of the old Qualik's face moved together, and he smiled at this younger woman who sat across the fire from him.

"My grandmother taught me that," said the woman, feeling the need to explain. "She lived here a long time ago. Near here, actually. Not on this lake. In Port Nerka. She taught at the missionary school."

Outside their sheltering tarp the rain fell unabated; the wind blew as before. Whisps of warming steam rose from the old man's blanket as he sat next to their fire, silently looking at them.

"How come you speak English?" asked the girl suddenly. "Why don't you talk in your language?"

"What do you know about our language?" asked the old man.

"Nothing."

"Then you know why I speak English to you."

"No, I mean who taught you?" the girl went on.

The old man let his eyes drift from theirs into the fire, and he kept them there for what seemed a long time before he answered. "Your great-grandmother taught me."

Across the campfire, the three family members stared at him, perplexed. The woman spoke first:

"How could you even know who we are?" she asked.

"Because it is who you are," he answered.

The girl looked at her mother. What does that mean?, her eyes asked. The woman had no answer for her.

"You knew Great Gramma?" asked the boy. "For real?"

"When I was young, she was our teacher," he answered. "She taught us many languages."

The woman looked carefully at the old man. It was hard to tell how old he was, but he might have known her. Even so, he was wrong about what she had taught at the mission school. Her grandmother had taught only mathematics during her whole lifetime, a career that the woman herself had chosen to follow early in her own life and one that she had then augmented through years of higher education before earning the position she now held at her home university as an associate professor teaching particle physics and quantum field theory.

"My grandmother never taught languages," she said cautiously. "You may not remember, or you may be thinking of another teacher."

"I know the woman who is your grandmother," said the old man. "She taught here, and she taught in many languages."

The old man's tone was so direct and certain that the woman found herself striving to keep the irritation out of her own voice. "Did she? And what languages were they?" the woman asked.

"All of the usual ones," answered the old man with equanimity. "But she liked numbers the best."

The boy and girl laughed and looked at their mother. "So does my mom," giggled the girl. "She teaches that language, too."

The woman smiled with her children. She hadn't expected a wisecrack, and such a deadpan one at that. Maybe he had known her grandmother after all.

The old man didn't smile; he hadn't meant to make a joke. "What stories do you use the numbers to tell?" he asked the woman. "The same ones your grandmother taught to us?"

"Numbers don't tell stories," said the boy, still giggling.

The woman ignored what her son had said. Instead, she concentrated on the old man, choosing her words carefully so as not to offend him. "No," she said. "The stories she told you were called 'arithmetic'. Mine are much more complicated. They're called 'physics'."

The old man nodded slowly.

"I have heard about the physics stories," he said. "I have heard that they are about the sun and the moon and the stars, and they are about things that are so small that no person has ever seen them. I have heard that the physics stories can tell about everything that ever was or ever will be, and that you can tell all of these many stories in exactly the same way, with just the number language."

"You have heard more about physics than I would have guessed," smiled the woman. "What else have you heard?"

"Just this," answered the old man very seriously. There was no smile on his face. "I have heard that you teach these stories even though you don't know they are true."

The woman worked to keep the smile on her face, not wanting to believe that this old Qualik man meant to be as rude and confrontational as he sounded. Perhaps it was just his directness of speech, a habit of the North Coast people that her grandmother had so admired.

"And where did you hear something like that?" asked the woman lightly, deciding that the insult had been unintentional.

"From your grandmother," said the old man, not taking his eyes from hers. "Just as she always told it to you."

The smile left the woman's face. The accuracy of what the old man had just said was so literally stunning that she felt suddenly lightheaded, and she found her hand reaching reflexively toward her grandmother's old amulet hidden under her shirt, trying to touch something solid and connected, the way a seasick person does on reaching dry land.

"How could you know that?" she asked, almost in a whisper.

"Because it is true," he answered steadily.

The woman waited to hear more. No one but she and her grandmother had known anything about this conflict, the only fence that had ever come up between the two women, the one that had steadily grown without even a gate until the day the old lady had died. The one that still hung between the woman and her grandmother like chainlink, separating her from the loving memory she could see, just out of reach on the other side; the joyous remembrance she so fervently wanted, and that she had traveled all this way hoping to begin to regain. Beneath her shirt the little salmon amulet seemed to grow heavier and hotter until the woman realized she was pressing it too hard with her hand, so she relaxed her grip. But she didn't let go.

She stared at the old man intensely, waiting to hear more. But he just looked back at her, and it was plain that he was not going to say more.

"I think you need to tell us who you are," she finally demanded. "And why you are here."

The old man looked at each of them, letting his eyes rest on theirs, each in turn, one at a time. The small fire between them crackled, flared and then settled, sending glowing embers up and away, out over the lake that tossed and churned in the darkness, unsettled and driven by an invisible wind. The old man leaned forward.

"I am like you," he said as the orange glow of the fire lit his face. "I am a story being told."

he first pure rush of totally fresh water struck the sockeye as she funneled with all the others into the open mouth of the flooding river. Here the current was steady and strong, the bottom deep and the water itself a milky, chocolate brown from the millions upon countless millions of tiny granules of silt and mud that had been washed into the river by the upstream rainstorms, and which now churned chaotically in the rushing tumult.

The gill-clogging turbulence made no difference to the salmon. Undeterred by the current and not in the least disoriented by the blinding murk, drawn by a force that fueled itself from a lifetime's accumulation of unspent energy inside each fish, the pod surged directly into the strengthening flow of water, pulsing themselves upstream.

Not one of the salmon would ever eat again, a moment that passed without their knowledge of it. Committed irrevocably to the final direction of their existence, the sockeye salmon swam headlong into the miles of river that lay ahead, draining their individual lives against the endless flux, climbing together out of darkness toward the unseen clarity of a higher place.

In the morning the rain continued to fall. It was a light rain, closer to mist than to droplets, and it hung in the dank air underneath low clouds that completely obscured the hills around the family's campsite. The wind had died away sometime during the night and the smoke from their newly started breakfast fire rose straight up before fading quietly into the overhead gloom. The woman and her daughter sat beside the fire with cups in their hands; the girl had hot chocolate while her mother sipped tea. There was no sign of the old Qualik man, no indication that he had even been there. Last night he had gotten up from their fire after speaking to them and had then gone out into the stormy night, vanishing back into it as mysteriously as he had first appeared.

After he had gone, the woman had spent a troubled and restless night alone in her tent while the children slept peacefully in theirs. Who was this strange old man, who not only remembered her grandmother, but who seemed to know things that had happened privately between the two women long, long after the grandmother had left Alaska, never to return? Had they corresponded? And if so, why had her grandmother never mentioned it? And how, even more unsettling, had he known about the disagreement between them? The unclosed gap that had brought the woman all the way here to try finally to bring together, if only in her own mind.

"You have become too literal, my dear," her grandmother had increasingly said. "Too scientific, if you will, and much too unforgiving. It's not what I expected you to be when you were a little girl."

"Only in my work," the woman had answered in defense. "I have to be rigorous, don't I, just as you always taught me to be? It's how I got where I am now, and that's pretty far, isn't it? How can I be too literal in grading physics exams? Should I give — what? — partial credit for two times two is three?"

"That's not what we're talking about, is it?" her grandmother had always chided. "Don't you see that you've let all that precision and proving affect the rest of your life? That you apply it now in places where it simply should not be? Don't you see that you're requiring it too soon from your own children? It's not right, my dear. It really isn't. It's certainly not what I did with you, and I don't want you doing it with them. Let them have some choice in their lives."

"They have more choices than you and I ever did," the exasperated woman would reply. "All I do is try to help them avoid the bad ones. It's my job."

"But that is the problem, my dear," her grandmother had said. "You treat it the way you teach your physics courses, by rewarding only their correct answers, not the process that gets them there. You need to give them more room for error, for experiment, and for imagination. But you don't because you no longer give that to yourself. And that, my dear, is wrong. It really is."

Her husband had become increasingly irritated at the woman for even listening to her grandmother's point of view on her career. "It's not about the kids and you know it," he said. "It's about you. She always prided herself on being such a great teacher, and already you've surpassed her in every way. You're a better teacher than she ever was, and it's precisely because of the rigorous standards you impose on your students. Next year you can have a full tenured professorship and I really don't think she wants you to have it."

That much was true, even if the woman hadn't wanted to acknowledge it. Her grandmother didn't want her to get the academic recognition she had worked so hard for, and the woman could not understand why. It couldn't be jealousy, she was certain: Her grandmother had always been the least selfish person she had ever known. It was something else, something that her grandmother seemed unable to make plain: "If you can't see it, it's because you won't allow yourself to," was what she would say. "It's what you've made yourself into by giving up what you used to be."

"Let her say what she wants," her husband had said in the most caustic argument they had. "But she has no business bringing our kids into it, and you have no business letting her do it. They're just simply not hers to worry about. The world they'll have to live in is not the one she grew up in. She's about to leave it, anyhow, and I'll be glad to see her go!"

The harshness of that last remark was what had driven the woman from her house in tears in full view of their children. Her husband had come immediately out to her and apologized, and she had accepted it. After that, they never let their discussions of the old woman degenerate into the sort of emotional warfare that neither of them wanted in their marriage. They promised each other never to let it happen again.

But in order to maintain the truce with her husband, the woman had drawn back from trying to resolve the contention that still separated her from the seamless relationship she had always had with her grandmother, and the gap remained open and never far from their conversations, even the easygoing ones that they had on Sunday evenings by telephone in the last months before the old woman had died.

It wasn't until one of their very last talks that her grandmother had told the woman that in her will would be a request. "It will be something that you can do, and the instructions will be explicit," the now-frail old woman had said over the telephone. "So I want you to promise me now that you will do it."

The woman had given that promise, without reservation and with her whole heart, and when it turned out to be this journey with the old woman's ashes to an unnamed green lake in Alaska with his children, her husband had been incensed.

"Even dead!" he had ranted. "Even dead she makes demands! It's too much. You can't do it. The department won't stand for it. It'll cost you the professorship if you miss classes for a camping trip! And I absolutely will not let you take the kids. They can't miss school at their ages. We're both teachers — it goes against every example we've ever set!"

But the woman was immovable. Her grandmother was dead forever, and she had passed away with the fence that had arisen between them still standing. All that was left for her to try to bring it down was this last yet-to-be-fulfilled promise, and she was absolutely going to keep it, no matter how mysterious it was, and even if she had to bring her children along in order to accomplish it. The children would be in no danger, she told her husband: Their great-grandmother would never have allowed that, and if he was worried, all he had to do was to come along with them. He knew that there was no real danger, even if he wouldn't admit it in the heated argument over their inclusion in the trip; it was what tipped the balance for him, though, finally. In the end he knew he had no real ability to stop her from going, short of putting their marriage itself on the line, something neither one of them would ever do. In the end, then, they had simply stopped arguing out loud about it, letting the disagreement hang in the space that it had opened between them, and together they had got the children ready for the trip, culminating in that last clear night in their back yard, searching the night sky for the North Star.

In her sleeping bag last night, the woman had clung to that memory while she ran her fingers over the old beartooth amulet in the dark. As her thoughts drifted, she found her fingertips traveling over the smoothly worn edges in a soothing, unbidden stroke that she slowly began to recognize as the exact pattern that she had so many times watched as her grandmother's fingers traced subconsciously over this same tiny salmon when she had worn it. Tears came to her eyes, but they were warm; the woman had even smiled, alone in her tent in the dark.

And with the warmth of that memory, sleep had finally come, fitfully, claiming the woman's muscle-deadened body well before it began to erode the edges of her consciousness as she let her mind roll unhindered into it, and toward another day. Ahead lay the keeping of an unmet promise to her grandmother, behind lay the breaking of one to her husband, and somewhere in between was a mysterious old man from a time long before she was born. A man who seemed to know both too much about her and far too little at the same time, as if he were someone else's interrupted dream dropped accidentally into one of her own.

Down by the water's edge, here in the dreary morning light, the boy was once again throwing small stones into the lake. Even in the dull gray overcast of this darkened day the lake water was a sparkling light green, clear as tinted glass in the near shallows and cool to the touch. When he threw his stones into the water, the boy could then watch them as they sank under the splashes they made, wobbling down through the green crystal water and coming to rest on the pebbled bottom. There the boy would concentrate hard, trying to keep his eyes focused on the one stone he had just thrown and which now lay among thousands of stones just like it on the bottom of the lake. As long as he didn't look away, as long as he kept that one stone fixed in his gaze, the boy could continue to see it clearly, but try as he might not to, as soon as he blinked the stone was lost to his sight forever, commingled and disappearing among all the others that had come to rest on the bottom of the green lake. Trying again, the boy reached for another stone.

Cr-r-uck! came the call of a raven from somewhere above, out of sight in the low overcast. The boy looked up, saw nothing but clouds, then turned toward his mother and sister as they sat by the fire. *Cr-r-uck!* came the call again.

"It's the Indian man," shouted the boy, running back to the other two and dropping the stone. "He's coming back!"

His mother smiled at him and his sister shook her head. "It's just a bird," the girl said to her brother.

"Uh uh," insisted the boy. "It's the Indian man. He's magic, isn't he, Mom?"

"I don't think he's magic, darling," soothed the woman to her son. "I think we just don't really understand him."

"I think he's magic," pouted the boy. He turned back to look for the old man, wherever he might be. In the glooming gray mist and light rain, none of them could see more than a hundred yards down the beach in either direction and only for the same distance out into the lake. There was no one in sight.

"If he's so magic," asked his sister, "how come you almost drowned? He didn't do anything. It was Mom that saved you, you know. Not him."

The boy kept looking away, trying to pay no attention to what his sister said. "He's magic," said the boy. "And he's coming back. I know he is."

"That's great," said the girl, shaking her head at his turned back. "Show some gratitude, why don't you? It's only your life."

"That's enough, children," said the woman. "Let's think of something else to talk about."

The boy was unhappy now, and he picked up a larger rock that was on the ground next to the campfire. With all his might he threw the heavy stone toward the water, but it fell short, dropping with a thud onto the gravel beach. His sister stood up.

"Here, let me try," she said. She picked up a rock of the same size, reached back and threw it hard toward the water. Splash! It just reached the edge of the lake, surprising even the girl.

"Wow," she said and turned to her mother with a grin. "Did you see that, Mom?" she asked.

"You almost hit the Indian man," said her brother behind her. "Look."

Coming out of the fog that covered the lake, heading straight across from where his own camp lay hidden, the old man glided toward them in a graceful, narrow wooden Qualik canoe, its sharply upswept bow cleaving silently through the stillness of the green lake. Carved onto its bow was the stylized eye of a raven and the sides of the canoe were painted with a deep red and a rich dark green that matched almost exactly the spawning colors of a mature sockeye salmon.

Beaching his canoe, the old man stepped out and walked toward the family. His dark blanket was wrapped over his shoulders, and hanging down over the outside of it lay his long unbraided hair, jet black with streaks of gray that matched almost exactly the color of the mist from which he had just emerged. As he had the night before, the old man stopped a respectful distance away.

"There is something you must see," he said.

"Is it the salmon?" eagerly asked the boy. "Are they here? Are they here?"

The old man turned to the boy. "When the sockeye return to this lake, you will know it. You will not have to ask. The lake," he said, "will be alive."

As he had before, the old man then stood quietly, offering nothing more than what he had already said. When it became clear that he would say nothing without prompting, the woman did.

"What is it that you think we should see?" she asked. "Can you tell us what it is?"

"You already know what it is," he said.

The woman took a breath. Her reaction to his direct manner of speaking — insulting and dismissive if used by, say, a fellow faculty member at her university — was her problem, not his, and she knew it. Still, it took a constant effort to keep it in perspective while at the same time trying to restrain her vivid memory of his standing still on the streambank as her son lay drowning before him. She took another breath.

"There are so many things to see here," she said with a forced lightness. "And we have just arrived. Which one is it that you think we should see?"

"It is the story that you came here for," answered the old man. "There is nothing else."

It was too much. "Nothing else?" snapped the woman. "My son almost drowned here. Is that the story I came here for?"

"Now it is a part of it," said the old man calmly.

"And why didn't you make it part of yours then?" she demanded. "Why did you just stand there and do nothing?"

"It was the boy's story, and it was yours," explained the old man. "It was not mine to tell."

"Is that what I did?" said the incredulous woman. "Tell my son's story?"

"Of course," said the old man. "You are his mother. Every child's story is first told by his mother."

The woman shook her head in disbelief. "So," she said to the old man who seemed to think everything, even life and death, was just a story. "Because you are not his mother, you were going to let a young boy drown?"

"No," answered the old man. He looked at the boy. "I was letting him try to tell the story for himself. If he could not do it yet, then I would have helped him."

The boy looked at the old Qualik man. "You would have saved me, Indian man," he said. "I know you would. Because you're magic, aren't you?"

The old man smiled at the boy, but he didn't answer. The woman wanted to tell her son that this old man certainly wasn't magic, he was just a superstitious and deluded old Qualik, but she held her tongue. There really was no point in hurting the old man; there would be plenty of time later to talk to the boy.

For a long moment none of them spoke.

"What about the story you said?" finally asked the girl, wanting to break the awkward silence. "Are you going to tell it to us?"

"The story will tell itself to you," answered the old man. "But first, you must tell yourself to the story."

"What does that mean?" asked the boy. "How do you tell yourself to a story?"

"You will see," answered the old man. "But first, we will have to climb."

"Where?" asked the boy.

The old man pointed up and away, toward where a hill rose at the top of the valley across the lake, hidden from their view by the thick overcast. "Above the clouds," he said. "Where the story waits."

he first freshwater rapids she encountered were gentle and invigorating to the salmon. Behind her forever now were the wide, deep, and turbid waters of the lower river. Up here the silt-cleansing effect of the water straining downhill through miles of gravel was swift and efficient. The female sockeye entered the rapids with all the swimming others and in three hundred yards she passed from a brown opacity into clearing waters that flowed faster and brighter than any in her adult experience.

With the tumbling, aerated current came a blood-charging jolt of freshly dissolved oxygen. In every tissue of her sleek body she carried the nutritional results of four years of nonstop feeding in the abundant North Pacific, and to the salmon it seemed suddenly as if every stored calorie had instantly triggered its own release. Jetting forward in response to this galvanic, internal explosion, the salmon shot ahead into the river current, bounced hydrodynamically upward from an underwater eddy, caromed toward the surface, flicked her tail and found herself suddenly and completely airborne. Frantically finning against thin air as her eyes registered indistinct blurs of forest green, cloud white and chocolate brown, she slammed back into the water and sank into the massed pod of salmon hugging the rocky bottom of the river. Reoriented and undamaged, the sockeye swam forward into the uninterrupted flow as the cells of her muscles recharged themselves, cycling upward toward their next explosive leap.

In the packed stream around the female salmon there was now a greater confusion of sounds and vibrations than before, a cacophany of sensations that meant nothing to her, that triggered no automatic responses in her as she pushed erratically through the milling throng of crowded, excited fish, regularly oriented by the incessant current of the river itself, and constantly swimming upstream.

A sudden crash somewhere nearby sent her and all the salmon nearby into an automatic, thoughtless surge of evasion, slamming into each other and pushing each other down onto the gravel or up into the shallows where the backs of some of the salmon came out of the inches-deep water as they frantically tried to swim with half their power wasted against thin air.

Another booming crash in the water sent the salmon thrashing on the other direction. The female sockeye felt herself pushed upward from below and she reacted with a jolt of pure propulsion that sent her skimming off the backs of fish below and once again straight out of the water. Fully in midair she finned wildly as she curved back toward the water, her view as before a meaningless blur of bright colors like nothing underwater, and she never saw the slashing arc of claws and fur from the streamside brown bear before they struck her on the back.

The narrow trail that led upward from the lake led the family into the forest of tall evergreen trees behind their camp, through an area of dense alders, and then out and along a small, flowing stream with grasses on both sides. The trail itself was pocked with the tracks of migrating caribou — double-moon-shaped hoof-prints that were wider than the boy's hand whenever he reached down to touch them.

The old man had told them to go ahead so that they would be in front, leading themselves instead of following him. The boy had, as usual, run to the front so he could be first, but his mother had called him back and took the lead herself. After his accident in the lakeside stream, she wanted to keep a closer watch on him from now on.

They climbed that way in silence for an hour, with the woman in the lead, the two children next, and the old man close behind. The trail was not steep, but it did traverse steadily uphill through the continuing gloom with no sign of clearing. It became even darker and so misty that none of the family members had noticed that there were no longer any trees along the trail. They were in open country now, above the treeline and the path had become even narrower and deeper, a dirt trail worn down into the pillowed, ankle-deep tufts of soft lichens and tundra that, if they could have seen, stretched away unbroken by shrubbery or trees in all directions.

"Are we inside a cloud, Mom?" asked the boy.

"I think we are," she answered without looking back. The trail was becoming steeper.

It began to grow lighter as they climbed. And then, in the space of just a few steps, they were in the clear. Above them the sky was blue, bright and brilliant, almost blinding. The hilltop lay just ahead of them, rounded and inviting, and they hurried to its crest. There, the family looked out and around. It was breathtaking.

Behind and below them the lake lay under a white shroud of clouds that filled the river valley for as far as they could see. Everywhere else, in every other direction that they scanned, the view was clear, the vista unbroken. Snowcapped peaks shone in the blue distance to the north; older, more rounded hills undulated away to the east, dropping from sight only with the curve of the earth itself; and far to the west, glinting, flat and endless, lay the ocean.

As the family stood and looked, the old man came up beside them and said nothing. For a long time no one spoke. Finally, he did.

"From this place," he said softly. "You can see the lake of the beginning."

The woman and her two children turned to look back toward the lake, far below. It was still obscured by ground fog and low valley clouds.

"I imagine it's beautiful," said the woman. "Will the clouds clear enough for us to see it?"

"You can see it now," answered the old man. "If you let it show itself to you."

"Can you see it?" asked the boy.

"Yes," answered the old man. "I see it now."

"See, Mom?" said the boy excitedly. "I told you he was magic! I told you! He can see through clouds."

The woman looked at the old Qualik man and took in a long, frustrated breath. "He's very literal," she said to the old man. "He thinks you really can."

"Yes, he can, Mom!" exclaimed the boy. Then to the old man: "Can't you, Indian man?"

"No, darling," she said to her son. "No one can see through clouds. If you can't see the lake down there, he can't see it, either."

The boy and the girl looked at each other. Something was going on between the two adults and it was unsettling. Their mother's gaze had turned to the old man and it stayed fixed there, waiting silently for his answer: She could employ that tactic as well as he. The old man was looking away from the lake, his eyes focused on the sky above the snow peaks, far to the north.

"Your mother is right," said the old man. "It isn't magic. I can't see through clouds any more than you can."

The woman nodded her head, then relaxed and took a breath. The tension was eased and the children could sense it. This was better.

"What is it then?" asked the girl. "If it isn't magic. What did you mean when you said you could see the lake?"

The old man slowly drew his eyes back from the northern sky. "You will have to decide for yourself what I meant," he said gently. "After you have heard the story."

"What story?" asked the boy. This was now much better.

"The lake of the beginning story," answered the old man. "The story that your great-grandmother heard when she was even younger than the two of you."

The old man turned his gaze to the woman. The woman looked back at the old man. Neither of them spoke, but the children could not miss that there was something important here, and it was about the story.

"Did Great Gramma tell you the story, Mom?" asked the girl. "How come you never told it to us?"

Their mother kept a steady gaze on the old man. "Your great-grandmother told me about the story only once," she answered. "One night when I was a little girl and we were all on a family camping trip. The northern lights came out and she said that one day I would go to a lake in Alaska where you could see the northern lights better than from any other place in the world. And when I was there, she said, I would hear a story, a very important story, even if she wasn't there to tell it to me herself. But she never took me here to Alaska, and I never did hear the story."

The old man nodded at the woman. "She has brought you here now," he said. "And if you will listen, there is a story. A very important story."

The woman waited before answering, thinking of how exactly she should answer the old man, but there was only one truthful way. Still, she hesitated.

The children looked back and forth at the old man and their mother.

"Will you tell it now? Please?" implored the boy.

"I want to hear it, too," added the girl.

The children looked to their mother, afraid that she would tell the old man not to tell it.

"Why not?" said the woman at last, keeping her eyes on the old man. "We do like stories, don't we, kids?"

The boy and girl smiled at their mother. She had read them stories almost every night when they were younger. Secretly, both of them wished that bedtime still did, at least sometimes, include a small fable read out loud by their mother from a familiar book.

"Yeah," said the girl with a wistful look toward her mother. "We like stories. We like them a lot."

The children turned to the old man, expectant.

"Then I will begin the story while we walk back down from here," he said. "But it is a long story. We will not finish it today."

"How about after dinner?" asked the boy. "Okay?"

"No," answered the old man. "Not even by your bedtime."

"Then when?" asked the girl. "Tomorrow?"

The old man started down the hill, leading the way this time. "Only the story knows when it will end," he said. "For now, we can only begin it."

Together they began the long hike back to the green lake. And the old man began the lake of the beginning story.

THE LAKE OF THE BEGINNING STORY
How There Came to Be Five Different Salmons and the Rainbow Trout.

In the beginning, there was only one ocean and one land. There were no rivers and there were no lakes. Just the ocean and the land. In the waters of the ocean there swam only one race of salmon. They were all the same and they always stayed together. The great ocean was so big that, no matter how fast or how far the salmon swam, they never found the shore. If there was any land on the earth, the salmon knew nothing about it. But the salmon were sleek and silver and very strong and they didn't care about anything that they had never seen. In the great ocean they were happy, and they swam wherever they wanted to go, whenever they wanted to go there. They loved their ocean, and their ocean loved them.

Then one day a storm came. It was a great storm and it stirred giant waves on the ocean, and the salmon had to dive very deep to avoid being thrown around and to stay together. But they were strong and they stayed together, and while they waited far, far under the surface, they heard a distant sound and felt a great shock that traveled through the whole ocean, reaching even the salmon as they hid from the storm, deep down and far away from whatever had happened.

The salmon were afraid for the first time in their lives, and they waited near the bottom of the sea, swimming in close circles together and wondering what to do. They wanted to get away from this stormy part of their great ocean. They wanted to get back to where the ocean had loved them, to where it was calm and safe, to where the sun shone above and the water was warm, but they didn't know how. All they could do was hide.

Then one day they heard their old ocean calling to them. Where are you? called the old ocean. Please come back to me.

A Fable of Salmon, Northern Lights and an Old Promise Kept

Then the salmon knew that they would be safe if they could get back to the old ocean. So, staying very close together, they swam off, headed in the direction from which they had heard the old ocean calling for them.

After swimming for many days in storms that would not stop, the salmon came to something they had never seen, something huge, dark and fearful that blocked their way for as far as they could see in either direction.

A giant tree, as wide as the whole world, had fallen across the ocean, cutting it in half.

The salmon stopped in confusion. First they swam one way, and then they swam the other, but all they found was the giant tree trunk blocking their way.

Then they swam in just one direction for many, many days, but still their way was blocked. Finally they came to another thing they had never seen: Land. It was the edge of the ocean that they had never seen.

In a panic, the salmon swam all the way back in the other direction along the giant fallen tree. For many, many days they swam, trying to get around this terrible wall, until they reached land again, this time on the other end of the giant tree.

They were trapped. The tree had fallen across the entire ocean, and they could not swim past it. The salmon couldn't get back to the other side of the ocean. They couldn't get back to where it was calm, quiet and safe. They couldn't get back to where their old ocean waited, still calling to them.

Where are you? called the old ocean to the salmon, over and over again. Where are you? Please come back to me!

The old ocean yearned for the salmon to come back, and when they did not, the old ocean was so saddened that it began to cry. So hard and so long did the old ocean cry that its tears formed lakes on the land where there had never been lakes before. Still the old ocean cried, filling the new lakes with so many tears that they overflowed and the tears ran down the face of the land and they all came together to form a river that grew and grew into one great torrent of flowing tears.

THE LAKE OF THE BEGINNING

There had never been a river on the land and it didn't know where to go. First it went one way and then another, rushing through the land and making valleys and whitewater rapids, and then one day the river heard the salmon, calling to their old ocean.

Help us! called the salmon from their stormy new ocean on the far side of the fallen tree. Help us find our way home!

So the new river turned toward the sound of the calling salmon, flowing straight and strong. Soon it reached the edge of the land and opened itself directly into the stormy new ocean.

Out by the blocking log, all the lost salmon began to taste the sweet tears of their old ocean that had come down the river to where they were. With a bounding joy, they swam as fast as they could to the mouth of the new river, and then they swam up into it. They were so happy that they no longer called out to their old ocean for help. Their old ocean, they thought, had answered their prayers and had made a way for them to come home. And so they swam up the giant new river, the first time the salmon had ever done this.

But the old ocean didn't know they were coming. It had only heard them calling for help, and then it heard nothing. The old ocean thought they were lost forever now, and so it began to cry even harder. It cried so hard that its own waters overflowed and ran into the lakes that its tears had formed on the land. The lakes swelled over their banks and cascaded down into the streams, and the streams poured into the giant river, and the giant river flooded downstream and met the swimming salmon head on.

The salmon pushed as hard as they could against the great flood of tears, but it was too much for them. The salmon were all pushed back into the stormy sea. There they were afraid, and once again they began to call to their old ocean:

Help us! they called, even louder than they had called before. Help us find our way home! Please help us! The river you made is too strong for us!

The old ocean heard them calling again, and then it realized that the salmon were trying to come home up the new river it had made. The ocean stopped crying, and the rush of tears down the new river stopped being too strong for the salmon.

So once again they swam up the river, and it was easier this time. But something had happened. Something had changed. The flood had been so forceful that it had carved through a mountain and now there was a waterfall across the river. It was the first waterfall, and the salmon didn't know how to get past it. None of them knew how to jump, for they never had to do this in their old, calm ocean. In great and growing confusion, they held in the river below the falls. None of them knew what to do, or where to go, or what would happen next. They began to argue with each other, something they had never done before. Some of the salmon began to call out to the old ocean, but others stopped them:

"Do not call out!" they demanded, "It was the calling out that brought the flood, and it will bring it again!"

"But we must call out to our old ocean," insisted the ones who had. "It was the calling out that brought us this river and it is the only way home."

Back and forth the salmon argued, but they could not agree on what to do. Always they had done everything together, and they knew that this must still be the way for them to be. But now they could not agree on what that way should be, and so they stayed in the river, stuck at the base of the waterfall, squabbling and disputing and taking sides against each other.

Soon the whole summer passed by while they argued, and it grew cold. Ice formed on the river and it began to freeze. The salmon had to swim back out into their new ocean where it was now even stormier and more threatening. Frightened and lost, the salmon stopped fighting, for they knew that to survive they must move as one and stay together. This they did, and as winter fell white and still over the land, freezing its new lakes and its one new river, the salmon struck out to sea, swimming far away to the south where they hoped the water would be warm enough for them to survive.

"Is that the end of the story?" the boy wanted to know.

The family and the old man had finished their long hike down from the mountain where the old man had started telling the lake of the beginning story. Now they were back by the tents of the family's camp, and it was growing dark.

"Of course it's not," said his sister. She turned to the old Qualik man who had continued walking and was headed toward his canoe on the beach. "There's a lot more, isn't there?" she called to him.

"If you say there is more," he said without stopping, "then it must be so."

"Stay and tell it then!" called out the boy as the old man pushed his canoe toward the green lake. The clouds that had been so thick earlier were beginning to break up; patches of fading skylight showed through the widening openings above, promising a better day tomorrow.

The woman watched him go. Already she was feeling regret at the way she had reacted to him earlier in the day, before he had started telling the lake of the beginning story. Most of it was venting, she knew, a reflection of things happening in her life, not his. And she always had been annoyed by creation myths, simple stories that only in rare cases shed any light on what she knew to be the true origins of the physical universe. Usually they did just the opposite: deflected the inquiries of young minds by trivializing the fabulously complex interactions that she had devoted her adult life to examining and trying to explain.

But this myth was off to a better start than most she had heard, and the old man had told the story well, with animation and style, captivating the children and, she had to admit, herself, too, even as she kept her guard up against it misleading her children in any lasting way. She was, in fact, looking forward to his continuing it. But not now.

A Fable of Salmon, Northern Lights and an Old Promise Kept

"Let the poor old man go, darling," said the woman with her eyes on the old Qualik man as he got into his canoe. "I'm sure he needs to rest now. And you need to have your supper and a good night's sleep."

The old man began to paddle steadily away, his graceful little canoe barely leaving a wake as it glided silent and straight, skimming away from them on the unruffled surface of the green lake.

"Will you come back tomorrow?" called out the boy. "Will you, Indian man?"

The canoe moved away; the old man did not turn around.

"It's okay, darling," the woman said to her son. "He's an old man. I don't think he can hear you."

The boy turned to her. "Yes he did," he said. "Didn't you hear him answer?"

"I'm afraid not, sugar," smiled the woman. When the boy had been very little, first learning to talk, his mother would sometimes come into his room and find him talking to his stuffed animals. When she asked him what they were saying to him, the boy would act just as he did here on the green lake, turning to her with a quizzical look and wondering how come she couldn't hear the words for herself. Then she would smile and ask him this same question:

"Why don't you tell me, so we can both share it?"

The boy could tell that his mother didn't believe that he had heard something from the old Qualik man, that she was just continuing the game they had played since he was a little boy. But today he didn't feel so little any more. And besides, he really had heard what the Indian man had said to him, even though it had barely been above a whisper and the old man hadn't turned around when he spoke. The boy looked at his mother and shrugged.

"Forget it," he said. "It didn't mean anything anyway." The boy picked up a stone and threw it half-heartedly toward the water. His mother watched him, and realized that she had made a mistake.

"Hey," she said softly to the boy. "Look at me, darling."

The boy turned to his mother. There were tears in his eyes. "I'm sorry, sugar," she said. "He did say something to you, didn't he?"

The boy nodded his head and swallowed the lump in his throat, sniffed back the tears and took a deep breath. His mother wanted to go to him and take him into her arms, but she held herself back. This was a pivotal moment between them, and she wasn't sure how to handle it.

The boy looked back across the lake. The old man in the canoe was gone from sight. The lake was as smooth as if nothing had crossed it. Everywhere it was quiet; the night began to darken the valley around them. The boy turned back to his mother.

"What did he say, darling?" she asked. "Is he coming back tomorrow like you asked?"

"I don't know, Mom," the boy whispered. "I don't know. What he said didn't make any sense."

"What was it?" she asked. "Maybe I can understand it for you."

"He said that it didn't matter if he came back or not. From now on, the story would tell itself to us." The boy looked at his mother with nothing but questions in his eyes. "How can a story do that, Mom?"

The woman looked at her son, and she felt her antipathy toward the old man coming back with a rush that surprised her with its strength and suddenness; her ears actually burned and she could feel a surge of pulsing blood in her head. Why did this old man keep having this effect on her? Was she overreacting because her own children were involved, or was it just her? She turned away from the boy and looked across the lake into the gathering darkness.

"It can't, darling," she said quietly. "Stories are invented by people, and he invented this one. He'll be back to finish it."

An hour later, after they had gathered more firewood and set about preparing their evening meal, the old man reappeared, paddling across the lake toward them in his canoe.

"It's the Indian man!" cried the boy.

His mother looked up to see the old man coming. "Go into the kitchen duffel," she said to the boy. "Get out another supper dish."

The old Qualik man beached his canoe and walked toward the family. The boy came running back from under the tarpaulin, carrying an aluminum dinner plate.

"It's for you, Indian man," grinned the boy. "Mom wants you to eat with us." He handed the plate to the old man, who took it in both hands and then looked at the woman. She nodded her head.

"You surprise me," he said. "I did not think that your heart had much generosity in it toward me."

"I know something of your customs," she said to him as an answer. "I knew you would be back to continue your story, so I have invited you to share our fire and our food before you do."

The old man set the plate down near the fire, then turned and walked back to his canoe. He reached inside it and lifted out a willow branch with four freshly killed rainbow trout hanging from it by their lower jaws, cleaned and ready to be grilled. These he brought back to the fire, where he stuck the end of the branch into the gravel so that the fish hung above the ground, free from grit and sand until it was time to cook them.

"I accept your kind invitation," he said.

The boy and the girl came quickly over to inspect the fish. Each was about a foot long. Their backs were copper-colored with a blush of dark green, their underbellies a creamy white, and along each of their sides was a wide, red slash running from their gill plates to their tails. Fine black speckles were scattered over this whole color scheme that really did look almost like a rainbow.

"Wow," said the girl. "How can you kill something so beautiful?"

"Their beauty is for more than just your eyes," answered the old man. "The trout is beautiful in your stomach as well."

"I hope so," said the boy. "I'm hungry. I'm glad you brought four, Indian man."

The woman looked from her son to the trout and then to the old man. "Why did you kill four of them?" she asked carefully.

"There are four of us here," answered the old man.

"But you already had them in your canoe," pressed the girl. "How did you know to get that many before you got here?"

"I didn't know before," answered the old man patiently. "But when your mother asked me to dinner, then I knew. So I got them."

The two children looked at the old man, and then at their mother, trying to make sense of his answer.

"That answer," said the woman to him finally, "is something that I will explain to them after you leave."

The children looked back and forth. The problem between the adults was out in the open again, and they didn't like it.

"I don't want to talk about dinner," said the boy. "I want the Indian man to finish the story. Can you tell it some more, Indian man?" he pleaded. "Please?"

The old man and the woman said nothing as they continued to look at each other.

"I think it's a good idea," said the girl, looking at her mother and then at the old man. "Let's hear some more of the story."

Their mother kept her eyes on the old man. "Why don't you tell the story," she said after a pause. "Unless, of course, it prefers to tell itself."

The old man showed no response to this. Instead he calmly turned away from the woman and toward her children. Looking at them, he began the story where he had left off.

The lost salmon spent the long winter far to the south in the strange, stormy ocean, and when the days grew longer and warmer they swam together back toward the north. At last they came to the giant log that had fallen across the ocean, and when they reached it, they turned and swam along it until they came to the shore, and along the shore they swam until finally, almost exhausted, they reached the mouth of the river that had been formed by the tears of their old ocean.

"What do we do now?" they asked one another. "Should we try to swim up into it again?" None of them knew the answer.

For many days they swam in circles at the mouth of the river, and then one day they heard their old ocean calling to them, just as it had the year before: Where are you? it called. Swim up the river I have made! Come back to me!

The salmon were filled with joy and they all swam into the river and hurried together up into the fresh water. For two days they swam as hard as they could, and they didn't even get tired, they were so happy to be finally on their way home. But then, just as the year before, they came to the giant falls. They were stopped, just like before.

"Oh no!" they cried to each other. "We are trapped again. What will we do?"

"Let's try to swim up the falls," said some of the stronger fish. "We can make it."

The other salmon weren't very sure of this idea, but none of them had a better one, so together they all swam up under the waterfall, and then they tried to swim carefully up into it. The waterfall just pushed them all back into the pool below it. They got nowhere, and again some of them began to cry. Now they were sure that they would never get back to their old home ocean.

But this time some of the strongest and bravest salmon refused to give up. "Get out of the way!" they shouted. "Make room for us! We're going to make it!" So the other salmon got out of their way and the brave salmon swam far back in the pool, and then they turned around and swam faster and faster and faster until they got under the waterfall and then they turned and swam as fast as they could straight up into the tumbling water.

And then, just as fast as they swam up, the brave salmon came crashing back down inside the waterfall. The current carried them back into the pool, and the other salmon could see that they were bruised and battered from where the waterfall had pushed them down against the rocks at the bottom of the river. None of the other salmon wanted to try after they saw that.

But the strong and brave salmon didn't want to give up. "We can't swim straight up inside it," one of them said. "But maybe we can make it if we try to jump over it."

"No! No!" cried the other salmon, who were wiser and more careful. "You can't jump! Up in the air you can't breathe! Up in the air is where the fish hawks fly! They will catch and eat you! You have to stay with us! That's how we have always protected each other!"

The strong and brave salmon thought about the dangers and they knew that the wise and careful salmon were right, but the strong and brave salmon decided to try it anyway. Back they swam to the far end of the pool, turned around, and then, madly swimming as hard as they could, the strong and brave salmon swiftly turned up toward the surface in front of the waterfall and while all the others watched they shot up and out of the water.

They didn't come back.

The others waited, expecting them to crash back into the water, but they didn't. Nothing happened. The strong and brave salmon had all disappeared.

"Oh no!" cried some of the remaining salmon. "They've been eaten by the fish hawks!"

"Oh no!" cried some of the others. "They've landed on the dry ground! Now they can't breathe!"

"But wait!" called out a few. "What if they did make it over the falls? Maybe we should try, too!"

"No!" insisted the wisest and most careful of the salmon. "They cannot have survived, or one of them would surely have come back to tell us that it was all right.

No. They are gone forever."

And then the salmon were all sad, and they grieved for their lost companions who had been so strong and so brave, and who were now gone forever. Disheartened and resigned to their fate, the salmon swam in circles below the falls until once again it became cold, and ice began to form, and they had to swim back out into the stormy new ocean. Winter came, and the remaining salmon swam back to the south, trying to stay warm and wondering what would ever become of them all.

The boy got up very early the next day and waited all morning for the old man to come back and continue his story of the lost salmon, but he did not; across the lake there wasn't even a sign of his campfire. His mother told the boy that that he was forbidden to walk around to the other side of the lake to try to find him.

"He will come if he wants to," she told her son. "Don't you go looking for him. I want you near here where I can know that you're safe."

At noon the woman went to her tent, took out a small, handheld radio and made her required call to inform the air charter service that all was well. She told the dispatcher that they had met an old Qualik man who was camped across the lake, and the dispatcher had said that was fine, but not to count on him if anything happened. "We know who he is," crackled the voice on the radio. "He comes and goes, so you may not see him again. But don't worry if you do. He's just a harmless old man."

The woman told the dispatcher that she had already decided that for herself, and said that she would call back tomorrow or the next day.

"Roger that," said the dispatcher through static. "Reports from the coast say that the salmon came into the river night before last. Couple of days and you should see them in the lake."

"Oh good," replied the woman into the speaker. "We really should start traveling on Friday if we're all to get back to school on time." Then she signed off and put away the radio.

The boy was sitting cross-legged beside the smoldering campfire, stirring the coals with a stick. The woman walked over and sat beside him. She gave him a kiss on the top of the head.

"The radio man said that the salmon are on the way," she said. "Someone saw them down in the river."

The boy stirred his stick through the dwindling fire, sending up a small cloud of ash and smoke.

"Mom?" said the boy, "are Great Gramma's ashes like these?"

"Yes," answered the woman. She had long ago learned to be ready for his unexpected questions, and to answer them as directly as she dared; it was usually what he wanted. "I think they probably are."

"How come people get burned up when they're dead?" he asked.

"They don't always," she replied. "Some just get buried. It depends on where the people are from, or what their religion is, or a lot of things that you'll learn about when you get older. Great Gramma wanted to get cremated, so that's what we did."

The boy thought about that as he continued stirring the ashes in the fire ring. His probing stick overturned a small unburned chunk of firewood and it flared with fresh combustion, erupting in a small upward billow that carried a cloud of ashes with it as it rose up and away from the woman and the boy. She put her arm around him and gave him a light hug.

"Maybe that's why she wanted it," said the woman. "So her ashes could float away, up toward heaven."

"But they won't," said the boy.

"Why not?"

"Cause they're not hot," he answered matter-of-factly. "They're cold."

The woman clung even tighter to her son, the physicist in her knowing exactly what to say and the mother knowing absolutely that she would not. Instead she just let the answer ache inside her as she held him, until finally she had to stand and look away while the feeling cleared. The boy got up and walked to the edge of the water.

"I want to explore, Mom," he said as he picked up a stone and threw it aimlessly out into the lake. "I want to look around. I don't want to sit here all day." The woman knew what her son really wanted, but she also knew that it was unfair to keep him right here near their own tents, something that she didn't much feel like doing herself. She thought about taking a walk, but she wasn't sure where the trails were.

"I'll get the topographic map and a compass," she said, turning back toward the tents. "We'll go for a hike."

Why don't we go look for the salmon?" suggested the girl. "Let's see if they're here."

"There's a good idea," said her mother.

The boy didn't think it was a good idea at all. "The Indian man said we would know if the salmon were here," said the boy. "He said the lake would be alive."

His sister shook her head at him: "You don't have to believe everything he says, you know."

"He knows way more than you," sneered the boy at his sister. "Way more."

"Enough, enough," calmed their mother. "Let's walk down the lake shore and see what we can see."

The three of them started out from their camp, walking on the beach in the other direction from the way the boy and girl had run to the old man's camp. The rocky beach was easy to travel on, and soon they began to find things that interested each of them. Bleached sticks of driftwood were all along the top of the beach, up against the grassy edge, and they took turns selecting one and saying what the weathered shape reminded them of. In the fine, wet sand right at the shore's edge were the tracks of birds in all sizes, mixed sometimes with the deeper imprints of caribou, moose and, once, the unmistakable print of a bear. The boy and girl turned wide-eyed to their mother.

"Are there bears at this lake?" breathed the girl.

"Yes, darling," answered. "Every part of Alaska has at least a few bears."

"Grizzly bears?" asked the boy.

His mother nodded. "But not many around here," she said. "It isn't really prime habitat for them."

"Cool!" said the boy. "I want to see one!"

"Not cool," said his sister. "You never said anything about bears, Mom. What do we do if one comes?"

"Nothing," said the woman. "If we don't threaten them, they won't threaten us. And besides, we really won't see one. They're very shy of people. They don't want to see you."

"But what if they do?" insisted the girl.

"Then Mom will shoot it. Won't you, Mom?" enthused the boy.

"No, darling," she said. "I won't shoot anything. We don't even have a gun."

"No gun?" asked the disappointed boy.

"No, darling," the woman answered lightly. "You know we don't even own one, and we've never had one on any of the other trips, have we?"

"But we've never seen a grizzly bear track on any of them," cut in the girl. "What if one comes?"

"Then I'll use this," smiled her mother as she pulled the salmon amulet from under her shirt. "It's carved from a bear tooth, and it's supposed to keep us safe."

"Yeah!" enthused the boy. "It's magic!"

"Mom!" cried his sister, on the verge of frustrated tears. "That's not funny!"

The woman tucked the amulet away and reached out to her daughter. "I'm sorry, honey. I know you're worried, and it's okay to be. But we really are safe here. The odds of our even seeing a bear are very, very small."

"But what if we do?" asked the girl.

"Then it will be up on one of these hills, far away from us, and we'll be lucky if we can even tell what it is," answered her mother. "Most people never get to see one in their lives, except in a zoo, so you'll have a good story to tell the other kids when you get back to school."

The girl certainly didn't think that seeing a bear would be lucky; not out here in the wilderness, all alone without a gun. She looked again at the bear track which, even to her untrained eye, seemed to be an old one.

"Let's go back to our camp," she said.

"No, darling," answered her mother firmly. "You should learn to control your fears, not let them control you. Especially when they really are groundless. This is a good place to practice it. We'll keep walking."

And so they did, continuing down the lake shore while the boy and the girl looked very carefully at the open tundra on the hills all around them.

"What's that sound?" asked the boy after they had walked for another half-hour along the green lake. The other two hadn't detected it yet, but as soon as they stopped and listened carefully it came to them: a distant noise that might have been the wind had it not been so steady, and had its volume not been so low and hissing at the same time. They all listened carefully.

"It's the river," said the woman when she finally recognized what it had to be. "We're getting near to where the river flows out of this lake."

And indeed they had done just that. Two hundred yards down the shore they found the lake's only outlet, a 25-yard-wide opening across the beach out of which the lake water ran as steady and smooth as an overflowing bathtub. Fifty yards out into the lake there was no visible flow; the lake surface was as placid as it was everywhere else along its shore. And even in the opening itself, where the current had to accelerate as it began to fall more steeply into the funnel of the draining outlet, the surface was equally smooth as it ran over the gravel where the three could see every stone on the shallow bottom, evenly distributed and unmoved by all the water moving constantly above them.

The boy picked up a rock and threw it out into the water near the outlet, wanting to try again to see it land among the other stones on this new part of the lake bottom. Splash! Instantly the stone and the splash itself shot away in the invisible current, sucked downstream and disappearing into the flowing outlet.

The boy's eyes went wide. "Wow!" said his sister. "That's strong!"

The woman watched her children react to the fast-flowing water, and she thought of a way to demonstrate something. Looking around, she spied a drift-wood spruce pole about ten feet long and thick as a baseball bat at its greatest diameter. "Pick up that pole, kids," she said. "I want to show you something."

The two ran and picked it up, and their mother told them to go up the beach, away from the outlet, and then to push the pole into the gravel a few feet out into the lake. They did. "So?" they said.

"Now do it closer to the outlet," said the woman. The children did, and this time there was enough current to push against the pole and make a small wake as they held in place.

"Closer still," said their mother. This time there was an even stronger current pushing against the pole, so much that the children had to lean hard to keep it in place.

"And one more time," said the woman. "Right in the outlet itself." She stepped closer to them to hold on in case one of them slipped, and watched as they tried to push the pole into the gravel under the fast current. They couldn't even get the tip far enough down to embed it in the gravel before the flowing water whisked it downstream, so the woman helped them. When the spruce pole was firmly stuck into the bottom, it took all three of them to hold it there as the inexorable current pushed against it, sliding it downstream as the tip dragged a trench through the gravel and water splashed steadily on the three people. Eventually they had to give up, and the current snatched away the spruce pole. Quickly it vanished downstream.

"It's like holding your arm out the car window when you're going fast," said the girl. "Only stronger."

"Way stronger," agreed the boy.

"This is different," explained their mother. "It's called Bernoulli's Principle and it's what makes water go faster through a hose nozzle and it's even what makes a wing lift an airplane. But what's important for us here is what it means for the salmon. Because Bernoulli's Principle says that if water flows through a tight place, it has to flow faster. It has no choice, and the tighter the place, the faster and stronger it has to flow."

The children liked the demonstration, but they never liked it much when their mother talked about physics. The woman, of course, was well aware of this; she knew when to leave theory and get back to applications.

"Now I want you to think about something," said their mother. "I want you to think about the salmon that have to swim from the ocean all the way to this lake. They have to swim against the current you just felt, and against currents even stronger, and they can't just let go like we did. Ever. Night and day and night and day and night and day. So when they get here, I want you to remember the stick that three of us could not hold against the current for even one minute. I want you to think about that, and about what each and every salmon accomplished just to get to this lake."

The children looked at their mother. She didn't usually speak this way to them, with such vehemence and intensity.

"And then," said their mother in a quieter tone, "I want us all to think about a woman who sent us all the way to this one place so she could be waiting for them when they arrived. I want us to be thinking about that great old woman who was so very young when last she saw the sockeye salmon, and who promised herself her whole life that she would see them again. And when the sockeye salmon do get here, and we do scatter her ashes into the water with them, I want us all to think of your great-grandmother, and of ourselves, and of your own children to come. I want us to think about promises, and how important it is to keep them."

The woman then looked away from her children, and out over the green lake. For a moment none of them said anything.

"I'm thinking about Great Gramma now, Mom," said the boy.

The woman and the girl turned to the boy. The family smiled at each other, but all three had tears in their eyes. With nothing left to say, the woman put her arms around each of her children and started with them back in the direction of their camp.

"Come on, kids," she said happily. "Let's go back and have dinner. Who wants to bet that there's going to be a strange old Qualik man who comes over later, ready to tell us some more of the lake of the beginning story?"

"Not me," said the girl. "I won't bet. He'll come over for sure. In his canoe."

Out over the lake, a lone raven flew, high and far away. *Cr-r-uck!* it called, and its voice echoed to them from the surrounding tundra hills.

"He's not a strange old man, he's a magic man," said the boy, looking at the raven. "And he's already there."

T hat second winter in the stormy new ocean was long and cold, and the unhappy salmon hardly ever saw the sun. Some of them even began to forget what it had been like in their old, warm ocean, for it had been so long since they had been in it, so long since they had tasted its sweet waters.

But just as it had the year before, spring slowly and finally came, and together the salmon set out to swim back to the north, back to the river where the other salmon had disappeared. This time, because they had done it two times now, they had no trouble finding the river. They swam easily to it, and just as easily they swam up into it, and once again they found themselves at the base of the waterfall. None of them had any new ideas, so once again they swam around and around, growing sadder by the day, even as the days themselves grew warmer and warmer.

Help us, old ocean! some of them cried out half-heartedly. Tell us how to get back to you!

Together they listened carefully, but there was nothing to be heard from their old ocean. Dejected and lost, they continued swimming in slow circles at the base of the waterfall. For days and more days they swam in circles.

"Look!" one of the salmon said one day, and all the others swam over to see what it had seen.

It was a tiny red jewel, round and soft, and it floated in the middle of the water, washing downstream in the river current. All the salmon swam alongside this strange new thing, fascinated by how small and perfect and red it was.

"What is it?" they asked. But none of them knew, none had ever seen anything like it.

"I know what it is," said one of the salmon. "It's food. Our old ocean has sent us some food."

"It can't be," said one of the wisest salmon. "Our old ocean would have sent more. This isn't enough for all of us."

The salmon who said it was food rushed forward and swallowed the red jewel before any of the others tried. "It's enough for me," said the greedy salmon.

"Look! Another one!" called out another salmon. But before most of them could get a close look at it, another greedy salmon rushed in and ate it. "It's enough for me, too," said the second greedy salmon.

"Where did it come from?" the wise salmon asked.

"It came down from the waterfall," answered the one who had seen it. The salmon all turned toward the waterfall and, as they watched, another red jewel came bobbing down in the current, so red that it seemed to glow in the water. One of the two greedy salmon rushed forward to eat it.

"Stop him!" commanded the wise salmon, and other salmon quickly blocked the greedy one's path.

"Something is happening," said the wise salmon. They all swam closer to see.

And so, while they all watched, the small, round, red jewel opened up and out swam a tiny, living salmon, so small that they could barely see it.

"A miracle!" cried one of the adults.

"A miracle for certain!" cried more of the adults. The adult salmon all turned to the wise salmon. "But what can it mean?" they asked.

"It is a spirit," spoke the wise salmon. "It is the spirit of one of our sisters and brothers who were so brave and who jumped over the falls last year. It is the sign that we have all called for. It is a sign that there is a way back to our old ocean, and it is up this river."

"A spirit," agreed the others as they joyously gathered around the tiny salmon. It was so small and so thin that they could see right through it as it swam in the clear water among them. "Yes! It is surely the spirit of one of our old friends who has come back to show us the way!"

"But wait," said one of them. "What about the other spirits."

Then the salmon all remembered what the greedy salmon had done: They had eaten the red jewels that carried the spirits of their old friends. The salmon turned with anger to face the two greedy ones.

"Please don't be angry with us!" pleaded the greedy pair. "We didn't know! Please forgive us!"

But the salmon did not forgive them, and they did stay angry with the greedy ones. So they took them and cut them and painted red stripes down their sides with their own blood, and then they chased them away and told them they could never be salmon again.

"Go," spoke the wise salmon to the outcasts. "You are marked forever with the red stripe of your greed. Find your own way in the sea, and find your own way in the river. From this day forever the red stripe will show that you are no longer one of us."

When the two greedy ones with their red stripes were gone, the wise one gathered the rest of the salmon together and spoke to them:

"The spirits of some of our brave brothers and sisters who went before us up this great river have been destroyed by our own greed and hunger. We have marked and driven away two of our friends forever because they were the ones who did it. But we must all remember that it could have been any one of us who ate the spirit-jewels, for we were all hungry and none of us knew what they were."

The other salmon reluctantly agreed, for they knew that the wise salmon spoke the truth. The greedy salmon had just been the fastest.

"This must never happen again," the wise salmon continued. "So from this day forever, the river will be a sacred place. Not one of us will ever again eat anything when we are in the river, for it is the place of our spirits."

All the other salmon solemnly agreed.

A Fable of Salmon, Northern Lights and an Old Promise Kept

"But now it is late," continued the wise salmon. "Winter will soon be here and we have no strength to get over this waterfall. Let us go back to the stormy sea where we can feed ourselves and get strong. In the spring we will come back, and we will try to get up the river."

And so, with great hope for what might lie ahead, the salmon all swam out to sea for another winter.

The old man finished this latest part of the lost salmon story long after dark. The sky remained clear, and all the individual stars began to shine, growing bright as pinholes in a black lampshade.

The children sat in silence, thinking about the old man's tale, while their mother set an aluminum pot of water to heat for dish cleaning on the grill she had set across the embers of their cookfire.

"We saw where the river goes out of the lake," said the girl to the old man. "Mom showed us how strong the current there is."

"Yeah," said the boy. "It's Bernie's something, and it makes it hard for the salmon to swim."

The old man smiled at the children. "The salmon are strong," he said. "They are even stronger than Bernie."

The woman smiled, too, and shook her head at her son. "It's Bernoulli, actually," she said to the old man. "He discovered a principle of the way liquid flows."

The old man nodded. "One of the great Western minds, then."

"Actually, yes," agreed the woman. "A Swiss mathematician in the eighteenth century."

The old man nodded again. "So he's the one who made the waters flow."

"No," answered the woman patiently. "The waters flow because of gravity and because they are liquid. Bernoulli was a scientist who discovered one of the laws that govern the way the waters flow. He didn't make them flow. They always flowed."

"According to the law?" asked the old man.

"According to the law," she answered.

Again the old man nodded. "How do you discover a law?" he asked. "If it is a true law, then does not everything have to obey it? And if everything has to obey it, then how can they if the law is not already known?"

The woman started to answer, but then she hesitated, recognizing the depth of the old man's question. She had spent years among academicians and theorists for whom an intellectual joust was both high entertainment and serious conflict, and she knew a deft debater's stroke when it nicked her. She hadn't expected anything like it from this old Qualik man, and it annoyed her to be caught so off guard. Why was it that every time she tried to relax and accept the old man for what he was, he did something like this to rekindle her annoyance at him?

"The laws that make the waters flow," she said coldly, "govern the interaction of a given force on the molecular structure of a specific liquid. For every different force, the liquid will behave in a specific way every time. That's a physical law of the universe in its present state and all water on this planet moves according to it. Bernoulli was simply the first human to discover its particulars. That's what I meant by 'knowing' the law."

The old man nodded. "I know that's what you meant," he said calmly. "It is the way of the Western mind to seek such certainties, and I have always admired it, just as I admired it in your grandmother."

The woman waited, knowing there was more. "But . . . ?" she finally prompted.

"But the Western mind is wrong," he said. There was no accusation or malice in his answer. No confrontation or invitation to further discussion.

"Oh, I see," said the woman. "Of that you are certain."

The old man smiled. "You speak with your own voice, but it is your grand-mother that I just heard."

"Was her mind wrong, too?" asked the woman. "Was it too Western?"

"When she spoke the number language it was," answered the old man, once again serious. "The Western mind is wrong because it speaks too much with the number language, and the number language is a very poor language because it can only tell one story, and that story is a very bad story. It is the very worst story ever told."

"What story is it, Indian man?" asked the worried boy.

"And why is it so bad?" interjected the girl.

"Because it is so hopeless," answered the old man. "And because it might be true."

The woman stared at the old man. Now she knew exactly what he was talk-ing about. For the first time since he had appeared, the woman physicist appre-hended the old man with every bit of her considerable intellect attuned. But it was too late. This old Qualik man had, she now fully realized, been leading up to this moment all along, and he had done it so masterfully and with such sub-tlety that not only had she not seen it coming, she had allowed him to include her own children irreversibly into the discussion on his own terms.

The children turned to their mother. "Do you know what story he is talk-ing about, Mom?" the girl asked.

"Yes, darling, I do," she answered, keeping her eyes on the old man. "It's a story called 'entropy'."

"Is it bad, Mom?" asked the boy.

Across the fire from her, the old man watched the woman carefully. Through the shimmering heat rising into the cooling night, his ancient eyes seemed to dance in the reflected firelight as he waited with her children for her answer.

It was an answer the woman did not want to give, the very one that had offered itself to her as she sat with her son, answering his questions about his great-grandmother's ashes: Entropy, the second law of thermodynamics, said that all matter and energy was inevitably and steadily growing inert. All heat had to grow cold. All order had to become disorder. Everything, every particle of every atom, would simply dissipate. Completely. It was, to her trained scientific mind, the ultimate truth. Everything living would die. Everything moving would stop. Everything held together would come apart. Nothing could possibly be immortal in a universe governed by the law of entropy. And to her mind, it was a law that had been proved.

But she also knew that the quest for continuing life is the green fuse that drives every living thing and is, for humanity, the source of all imagination and every dream. Without the hope of immortality, no civilization would have flourished over barbarism; selfless generosity would not have survived wars and famines; heartfelt prayer and the fear of God would never have tempered malice and greed; and not one person would ever have enjoyed time's most precious allocation, an innocent and blissful childhood.

"Is it a bad story, Mom?" asked the boy. "Is it as bad as the Indian man says?"

The woman physicist looked at her daughter, and then she looked at her son. "Yes it is, darling," she said softly. "It is indeed a bad story."

"Then I don't want you to tell it," said the girl.

"I don't either," said the boy.

The woman looked at them sadly, and then she looked at the old Qualik man. "I never meant to," she said. "It's the only story that truly will tell itself."

No one spoke after that, and the quiet seeped into each of them, even the old man as he picked up an unlit stick, produced a small knife from under his dark robe and absently began to whittle away some of the bark at one end. Firelight winked from the burning embers and all their faces warmed in the orange glow as the fire slowly burned down. Only one full stick remained unconsumed and then it too collapsed into the dying flames, sending up a small, soft shower of white-hot sparks before settling into the pile of still-burning coals. The woman put another piece of wood on the campfire and then got up and walked away from the light it threw as the fire rekindled behind her.

Down on the beach it was as calm as nights ever get, and as beautiful. There was no wind at all, and no moon; overhead the stars were so thick and bright that when the woman turned her eyes up to look at them it seemed to her that she could see them fully in three dimensions, some nearer and some farther away, a frozen cloud of thousands upon thousands of tiny perfect lights suspended against a darkness that vanished behind them in a hollow infinity of absolute black.

The woman's thoughts went out over the water of the lake, where the night sky was so perfectly mirrored on its glassy surface that only the line of distant hills separated the reflected stars from their twinkling sources above, and she found herself thinking about what the old Qualik man might have been like when he was young and her grandmother had known him. She wondered if they ever conversed, or if instead he had just sat mutely in the mission school-room, listening intently and saying nothing, nothing at all, while the young and earnest white teacher in front told all those stories in the number language.

Behind her, up by the renewed and brightening campfire, the woman heard her children's voices, and she knew before she turned to look that the old Qualik man had decided to finish his story tonight.

T he third winter in the stormy sea passed by quickly, for all the remaining salmon were filled with hope that when spring came, they would finally find their way up the river and back to their old, warm ocean. On the first day that the sun seemed to last longer, they all turned and swam directly to the river.

But the great river was not the same. It had changed during the winter. Now, where there had been one great river mouth, emptying into the sea, there were five separate smaller rivers, each flowing into the ocean in a different place. And swimming in all of the five rivers was a greedy new race of red-striped fish — their old outcast friends had become rainbow trout and already they had learned how to live in the new rivers, where they ate anything they wanted and stayed in the rivers all year-round.

The salmon stopped. Once again, they did not know what to do.

"Which one leads back to our old ocean?" some of them cried.

"Maybe they all do!" answered others.

"Maybe none of them do!" wailed some.

"Maybe some do and some don't!" worried still others.

"And what about the rainbow trout. They are not our friends!" fretted more of the salmon.

They swam in desperate circles, just as they always had done when they didn't know what to do. For days they swam this way, until one day the wise salmon called out and told them to stop.

"Stop, my friends!" he cautioned. "This will not do. We will waste the whole summer again. We need to start upriver now if we are ever to find our old ocean before the ice comes again."

"But how will we choose which river?" they all asked him.

"We cannot choose one," he answered. "Because we cannot know which one is the right one."

"But we have to choose one, so we can swim up it together!" insisted the others.

"No," answered the wise salmon. "We will have to do something else. Something that we have never done before."

"What is it?" they asked in worried voices.

The wise salmon looked at each of them. Each salmon was his old friend, for they had all been swimming together since the beginning of their time, long ago in their old warm ocean. Sadness came over his face as he slowly answered.

"Each of us will have to choose from the five new rivers. Each of us will have to decide which river to swim up into. We will have to divide and go separate ways from each other."

The salmon were shocked, and they all cried, "No!" Never had any of them even considered such a thing.

"But we are the same!" they insisted. "We have never been apart! We cannot go separate ways!"

The wise salmon felt the same way that they did, for he was one of them. With great sympathy and sadness he answered them.

"I know that we have always been together, and that when we were in the old warm ocean that loved us it was the best way to be, but now we are in a harsher place. The winters are long and very cold and we cannot live this way for very much longer. If at least some of us do not get back to our old warm ocean, then we will all perish and be gone forever."

The other salmon listened to the wise one, and they knew that what he said was true, for they could feel it themselves.

"So now each of us must choose," said the wise salmon. "And then each of us must go with those who have chosen the same way and stay with them as brothers and sisters just as we have always done together. We must swim up into the five separate rivers. We must be strong and we must be willing to jump the big waterfalls and we must never stop swimming until we get to the end of the river, just as the spirits of our lost friends have shown us to do."

The other salmon reluctantly agreed, for it was truly the only thing they could do.

"And above all," the wise salmon continued, "each of us must keep our solemn promise to the spirits of our old brave sisters and brothers. We will not do what our outcast brothers and sisters, the rainbow trout, do in the new rivers. Once we have entered the rivers, none of us will eat again until we get back to our old home, the great water of our beginning."

And so the salmon, who had all been swimming together since the beginning of their time, agreed to the solemn promise never to eat in the rivers. And then they turned toward the five rivers before them and each salmon made its own choice.

One of the rivers was bigger and faster-flowing than the others, and it was chosen by the biggest and strongest of the salmon, who selected it while the others were still deciding. These salmon swam up the big river and became Shawytscha, the King Salmon.

Then more salmon chose another river because it was much smaller, and they became Keta, the Chum Salmon.

The third group to choose wanted the river that was the clearest so they could easily see where they were going, and they became Kisutch, the Silver Salmon.

The fourth group was made up of smaller salmon who had trouble deciding which of the two remaining rivers to choose. Without thinking any more about it, they all went up one of them, and they became Gorbuscha, the Pink Salmon.

The rest of the salmon, who had been very unselfish and patient, and who had waited for all of their brothers and sisters to get the first choices, swam to the mouth of the one remaining river and together they swam up into its flowing waters. Because they had waited, the spirits of the old salmon blessed these last fish with

A Fable of Salmon, Northern Lights and an Old Promise Kept

the brightest red color of all the new races of salmon. They became Nerka, the Sockeye Salmon, and theirs was the only river that had a calm lake waiting for them at the end of their long struggle upstream.

The old man finished the lake of the beginning story as the last of the day's firewood collection had finally burned down so low that there was not enough light for him to see the children's faces. Nor could the children see his as he told it. Each of them was a darkened silhouette to the others as they sat without speaking, the only movement among them the measured strokes of the old man's small knife as he silently carved his stick in the dark. Eventually the girl turned and looked toward the beach.

"Wow," she whispered. "It's the northern lights."

For so long had they been facing each other across the fire that the children hadn't noticed what their mother had been watching as it slowly built in intensity across the celestial span: The aurora borealis had soundlessly ignited and now danced wildly in the northern sky.

Curtains of electric light blue and green floated across the silent fields of star clusters, rising and falling, fading and reappearing, blowing in the solar wind like diaphanous mantles of the gods. Columns of light pushed themselves up from the horizon, swayed like distant fountains lit by the neon lights of galactic cities, then faded away before rising again. Filaments of ghostly reds and glowing whites wobbled and shifted across half the night sky as eerie waves of spectral change pulsed intermittently through it all.

There wasn't a sound.

The children walked to their mother as she stood alone on the beach, watching. In her hands was the small package that she and her children had brought to the green lake, the ashes of her grandmother. Without taking her eyes off the display, she took their hands one at a time and placed them with her own on the package she held. Together completely now, the family watched the dance of the aurora against the northern sky.

"This is why you are here," said the old man behind them.

The woman said nothing in reply. She knew why she was here. The ashes in the small package had been softly calling to her from the moment the northern lights had begun to appear. Normally the woman would have shaken herself away from that sort of inner voice, something that she had always dismissed as a form of daydream, a distraction from the clearer thought that was her usual frame of reference for the world around her. But tonight she was tired, and she knew that this entire trip was about to reach its emotional climax; so she had allowed herself to heed the soft calling of the ashes in her tent, and she had gone quietly to get them as the old man finished his story. And now they were here, touched by her and by her children, calling still as the northern lights shone before them.

"What you are seeing," said the old man, "is a reflection. A reflection of what is over there, under the dancing lights."

"What's it a reflection of?" asked the boy. "What's under?"

"What does the dancing light look like?" asked the old man. "What do you see when you look at it?"

The boy and the girl kept their eyes on the lights, kept their hands on the package of ashes, while they thought about it. The girl took in a breath of sharp realization.

"It's a reflection of water!" she breathed. "It's just like water lights dancing on a wall when the water moves!"

The boy took his hand from the package and turned wide-eyed to the old man. "It's the old ocean of the salmon!" he said "Isn't it? It's over there, isn't it?"

The woman turned slowly to see what the old man would say. He looked her briefly in the eye; he looked at the two children. He handed the small piece of wood he had been whittling to the boy, and then the old man turned to the dancing lights, lifting his outstretched arms toward them as he answered.

"I only know what I want it to be. I want it to be the old ocean from the beginning of the world, the first water of all the salmon before they became separate races and had to go to different rivers. I want it to be the place where the spirits of all the salmon who ever lived have all gone. I want it to be the warm ocean that loved them all, that loves them still, whether they made it to the end of their rivers or not, whether they spawned and made new salmon or not, whether they ate or were eaten. For every salmon that ever swam I want the northern lights to be the great reflection of their own home that calls them safely toward the place they want to be."

The old man kept his gaze straight to the north. His ancient eyes were as dark as the night sky and in them the aurora danced. Slowly his arms came down to his sides.

"But I do not really know," he said.

For a long time after that none of them spoke. The northern lights grew brighter, dancing higher and higher in the firmament above and reflected so precisely on the mirrored surface of the calm lake that it seemed each glowing shard of light had a perfectly matched partner in the water, silently waltzing to the unheard music of the universe itself. The woman felt a tug on her sleeve.

"Mom!" whispered the urgent boy beside her. "Look!" She turned her eyes away from the soundless spectacle before them to look down at her son.

In his hand was the fresh wood carving the old man had just made: It was a tiny leaping salmon, two inches long, an exact wooden duplicate of the beartooth amulet that hung around the woman's neck, out of sight under her shirt. She looked up at the old man as both the sudden question and its plain answer cascaded over her in a warm flood of electric realization. The old man looked her steadily in the eye, silently confirming it.

THE LAKE OF THE BEGINNING

"When she was here," said the woman in growing wonder, "you weren't a boy, were you?"

"No," answered the old man. "I was a young man."

"And when she taught here, you weren't a student, were you?"

"No," again answered the old man.

"You were a teacher, weren't you?" said the woman.

"I was beginning to be," answered the old man. "In the way of the old people."

"And you used to come here, to this lake," said the woman.

"I have always come here, to wait for the stories to come here also. It's what you call imagination, and it is what I teach."

The woman looked closely at the old man, trying to see what was in his eyes, but he kept them turned away, shielded. It didn't matter; the story was already hers. She reached up to the leather thong around her neck and gently lifted the beartooth amulet out, took it off and held it out to the old man. His eyes came around to look at it.

The old amulet hung in the brilliant night air between them, barely moving in the crystal stillness as its miniature jeweled eyes caught light particles from the glowing aurora in the distance and returned them as tiny waves of every color that either the old man or the woman had ever imagined. Slowly the old man held out his hand, and the woman placed the amulet in it.

Tears filled his eyes as the old man gently held the beautiful little blue-eyed carving, tracing his weathered and deeply-creased fingers over the worn etchings from so long ago. The woman watched him as he completely lost himself in the amulet that her grandmother had worn for all those many years, and it took her breath away. In a voice barely audible, the woman finally asked her last question:

"She came here with you, didn't she?"

The old man looked one more time at the amulet, and then at the woman as he handed it back to her. He then turned toward the lake where the paired auroras danced in their mirrored, brilliant silence. There was no breath of wind, not a sound to be heard, and the old man's eyes were as still and glittering as the unrippled surface of the timeless lake that lay before them.

"Only once," he finally said, in a voice so quiet that the others could barely hear it.

And then, as his words whispered away from them, out and away into the night, there appeared a single bulge in the surface of the lake, out under the northern lights, as if a lone swimmer were pushing something round and smooth upward from underwater. The reflected aurora bent around the lifting surface tension, distorted by the change and appearing for an instant like falling light cascading down from the rounded, rising water and then the bonding friction gave way and a single sockeye salmon broke through the surface and rolled in the lake before all their eyes.

Off to the left another salmon rose and rolled, and then, farther out toward the lake's middle, another. From even farther out another sockeye jumped, coming clear out of the water, matched by one and then another leaper even before the first one had splashed back down. The lake seemed to erupt.

The entire surface of the lake began to break out with leaping and rolling sockeye salmon, so many of them that their splashing turned into a shifting, continuous hiss of nonstop thrown water as salmon appeared everywhere in showering jumps and subsurface boils, every one silhouetted and highlighted by the northern lights above them.

On the shore, none of the people moved, not one of them spoke. The sockeye salmon had returned to their green lake under the light of the silent aurora and there were no words in a spoken language that could add any clarity at all to the story that unfolded here before them, telling itself without knowing they were even there.

The water was dark as the female sockeye swam into the lake at the end of her long climb from the sea. Ahead of her in the calm water were thousands of salmon that had preceded her up the river, and the sound of their jumping and rolling came to her from all directions as she slowly finned out into calm water that, for the first time since she had left the ocean, did not flow against her.

Across her back were three shallow gashes where the flashing bear claw had slashed against her, white irregular streaks cut through the greenish red of her spawning colors, and they seemed to glow even whiter as she swam near the beach under the quavering northern lights that flooded down from above.

The salmon was not relieved to have reached the destination of her long journey nor was she inspired by where she was, sensations that were absolutely unavailable to her. That she had now arrived in the home waters of her birth was apparent to her only as a set of reactions that did not propel her away from them. Inside her were row upon row of tiny round eggs ready to be released and now she was in the place where it would happen.

For the rest of the long night, other salmon came up the river and into the lake, joining those already there and gradually reforming themselves into a pod not unlike the one they had been when they first approached the river. Turning in one direction, all the salmon began to swim in a slowly expanding circle under the northern lights, stretching themselves out against the shoreline of the lake until they ringed it entirely, thousands upon thousands of salmon endlessly orbiting the lake of their beginning. All night long they swam this way, slowly, steadily, continuously.

Morning came, and light flooded through the calm waters and onto the circling salmon. Cruising slowly around the lake with thousands of her kind in a widening gyre of living red and green and carrying with her the seeds of her own renewal, of all their renewal, the female sockeye swam in mindless peace toward deliverance.

It was morning on the crystal green lake and the woman stood with her two children on the beach, watching the spawning salmon as they circled the shoreline. Stacked neatly beside them were the duffels of all their gear that they had carefully packed at first light, and now they were waiting for the arrival of the float plane that would soon come to take them home. Standing alone a short distance away was the old Qualik man. Beside him on the beach was his carved and painted canoe, its salmon colors so accurately rendered that it seemed to have drawn them directly from the sockeye that swam endlessly past in the morning light.

Last night, under the unending display of the aurora, the woman had thought about the sockeye salmon, about what she was witnessing in the lake before her, and about what she knew from her studies and her reading. The "biological imperative," she remembered it being called, and she had now seen just how insufficient that phrase was in describing the undistracted force of life that drove the sockeye salmon directly and mindlessly to their own end, with no possibility of taking another path, even one that might prolong for any one fish its own individual existence.

The woman wondered what it was about the human race that had evolved into the one species on the planet that was, in fact, distracted. Why did people think, and why did humanity allow those thoughts to so often conflict with its own survival? What was it about the evolution of her own species that seemed to be such a radical and unlikely divergence from the developmental path of every other species that had now or ever before existed on Earth?

She thought about her own knowledge of physics, and how it was, as the old Qualik man had said, describable only in "the number language." And as she considered, it occurred to her that perhaps humanity did have a biological imperative and that it was just as unavoidable and directed as that of the salmon swimming upstream. *Homo sapiens,* it seemed to her, was uniformly driven by the quest for increasing awareness and a ceaseless desire for measurable truth, no matter where the trail toward its discovery took it, even if that final truth turned out to be the empty darkness of entropy, the absolute end of the entire universe before it collapsed back on itself and vanished into the void of naked singularity.

But if that were true, she continued in her own mind, if it is humankind's duty to follow the trail of scientific truth no matter even if the ultimate destination is despair and annihilation, then why is that imperative any different from the unalterable courses of all the other species, swimming upstream toward their own ending places? If humanity alone has a comprehending mind, then why is its apparent course toward something so mindless?

And, more important, she thought, does it absolutely have to be? Isn't there, at least theoretically, another possibility, a different current of thought not yet ascended? Can't there be, in fact, many other streams just as likely? And if there are, where do they lie? Ahead of us? Behind? Has humanity veered from the main river of its own salvation, or does that flow lie yet ahead, waiting?

The answer had to lie ahead, the woman concluded. The returning sockeye salmon knew which forks to take in returning to their upstream lakes, even if a few individual fish erringly turned off into dead ends. Humanity, too, was likely to be coursing toward the answers it sought. But there were so many beckoning choices, and the main river did seem so increasingly forbidding.

The answers for many, she knew, lay in religious practice, but theology had not provided the sort of answers that the woman physicist had sought. The conflicting dogmas of organized belief systems had, to her view, been responsible more for the disorder of civilization than for anything tending toward unity and had, therefore, seemed in perfect keeping with the law of entropy itself.

But the old Qualik man had hinted at another path altogether and last night under the northern lights the woman had allowed herself to glance down at it. In spite of the continuing animosity she felt toward him for the way he had so blatantly used magic trickery on her own children, the woman had sensed intuitively that there was something in the old man's story world that might reward unconstrained thinking. In the glow of the aurora, on the shore of the green lake, she had opened her mind to it.

What separates humankind from all the other living things on Earth, she thought, was just that: thought itself. The ability to consider things even if those things do not yet exist. Even if they have never existed. Or never will. Or absolutely cannot. The human mind, at least as far as it can tell, is the only living mind that can consider things beyond the dimension of dimensions themselves. And not only can the human mind do this, it seems that it has to do this, that it has no choice except to consider and to imagine and to reconsider and to imagine anew. Why?

What could possibly be the biological imperative in abstract thinking? What sort of cosmological river is humanity constantly swimming against and what could be the green reward at the end, swimming in a lake reached only by undiminished, relentless surges of countless individual human imaginations regenerated, reimagined and retold?

There was only one answer: It had to be something not yet fully realized. A story not yet completely told. A green lake of understanding perhaps not yet even imagined.

Last night, as the woman's thoughts brought her back around to where she stood on the shore of the lake with her grandmother's ashes in her hands, the perfect little amulet around her neck and her children standing beside her, she had finally come to understand why she was there, and what she was supposed to do with the ashes she had carried so far, and in so complete a circle. She had walked to the old Qualik man and handed the small box to him.

"Please take these," she had said to the old man. "She wanted you to be the one to scatter them into the lake."

The old man had taken the box of ashes and looked at the woman who had handed them to him. He said not a word, but gratitude was in his eyes and the woman had no need to hear him say it. The old man had then looked away as he held the box of ashes, and he let his eyes travel from the water before them and all the salmon in it up to the night sky that danced with the shimmering reflection of the brilliant aurora, the northern lights, up and over the horizon.

"Which lake?" he had asked very quietly.

The woman, too, had turned her gaze toward the water and the night sky. One more time she let her fingers travel to the amulet, dragging them lightly over the smoothed contours of what the old man had carved with such loving care so very long ago — the beautiful little beartooth salmon, the one with blue eyes. The one that had lept so high and had gone so very far away.

"The one she wants to be in," the woman had answered just as quietly. "The one that has called her back."

The droning of the approaching airplane gradually filled the valley around the lake, breaking the woman's reverie and bringing her back to the morning and to the present. The family and the old man could hear the airplane for long minutes before it actually appeared over one of the tundra hills to the west. Banking and cutting power, the little airplane dropped carefully onto the center of lake, skimmed easily across the placid surface, and settled, rocking gently before turning and taxiing toward the beach.

The woman and her daughter stood and waited for the float plane as it came toward them, but the boy jumped up and ran to the old man, who stood quietly next to his canoe with the box of ashes in his hands.

"Will you come with us, Indian man?" he pleaded. "Please?"

The old Qualik man looked down at the boy and smiled. "No," he said. "That place is your home, and it is time for you to go back to it. This is mine."

The boy looked back and saw that the float plane had reached the shore. His sister waved her arm at him, telling him to come back. The boy turned back to the old Qualik man.

"I don't even know your name," said the boy.

The old man looked at the boy. In his eyes the green water reflected, and the boy thought he could even see the red of the swimming salmon there too.

"My name," said the old man, "is Sammadug."

"Sammadug," repeated the boy, trying it out and wanting to remember it forever. "Sammadug. What does it mean?"

"It doesn't have to mean anything," answered the old man. "It is a name."

"But Mom says Ind—, I mean Qualik names always mean something," insisted the boy.

"Does she?" smiled the old man. "Then what does Caroline mean?"

"That's my mom's name," blurted the surprised boy.

The old man nodded. "It was your great-grandmother's name, too," he said.

The boy turned again to look at his mother and sister. Both were now waving at him to come back. One more time the boy turned to the old Qualik man. "I have to go," he said.

The old man looked at the boy, and then he reached out and lightly touched his head. "My name is Sammadug," said the old man. "And in your language it means 'Good Hope and Strong Will'."

The boy stared at the old man with wide eyes. He started to speak, but couldn't.

"Will!" called his mother from down the beach behind him. "It's time to go!"

The boy still stared at the old man. "But my name is Will," he said. "And my sister's name is Hope."

"I know," said the old man.

"Our names are the same as yours!" breathed the boy.

THE LAKE OF THE BEGINNING

"You see," the old man smiled. "Now you are beginning to tell your own story."

"No," insisted the boy. "It's my name. Will has been my name all my life."

"I know that," said the old man. "I always did."

"How could you always know that?" asked the boy.

"Because you just told me," said the old man.

The boy — Will — didn't know what to think, or how to react. Was the old man serious, or was he playing a game? Was he truly magic, or did he just want to seem to be, like his mother had said.

"I don't understand," said the boy finally. "How could you always know something that you just learned?"

"Because it is true," said the old man.

The boy knitted his brow as he tried to make sense of that. The old man continued. "Perhaps someday you will understand how that can be. Or perhaps not. It will be up to you to find a language that can tell a story like that. Or another story, one that no one has yet heard, one that you can tell so that then, after you tell it to them, everyone will always have known that it was true."

The boy concentrated hard now, knowing that this was not a game that the old man was playing. That this was the most important thing anyone had ever told him. In his mind he repeated every word the old man said to him, so that he could repeat them to himself later, over and over again, until he could understand them.

"Go now," said the old man to the boy. "Go with your mother and your sister. Go back to your home and find a place where you can go to wait for the stories, all of the stories, to come to you in a place where you can listen to them and where you can decide for yourself which of them is true."

The boy turned away then from the old Qualik man, and started back toward his mother and his sister and the airplane waiting to take him away, back to his home. He got halfway to the airplane and then he stopped and thought.

"Is this story true?" he called out as he turned around.

But the old man had disappeared, taking the box of ashes with him. On the beach was his canoe, and on the bow of the canoe, perched atop its own image carved into the upswept bow, was a raven.

Cr-r-r-uck! it spoke as it spread its wings, lifted off the canoe, and flew up, out and away, over the green water and over all the sockeye salmon that had once again returned to the lake of their own beginning.